THE COMING OF THE MONSTER

THE COMING OF THE MONSTER

A Tale of the Masterful Monk

By
OWEN FRANCIS DUDLEY

Problems of Human Happiness. V.

ST. AIDAN PRESS, LLC
Morning View, Kentucky

The Coming of the Monster: A Tale of the Masterful Monk.

First published in 1936 by Longmans, Green and Co., London, New York, Toronto.

Typesetting, layout and cover design copyright 2024 St. Aidan Press, LLC.

Cover and title page image from Freepik.com.

ISBN-13: 978-1-962503-10-5
ISBN-10: 1-962503-10-0

For more information, contact:
www.staidanpress.com
staidanpress@gmail.com

We have made no intentional change from the original text except to correct mistakes in spelling and punctuation.

AUTHOR'S NOTE

THIS present volume is the fifth of a series dealing with problems of human happiness.

The first, *Will Men be like Gods?*, is an answer to Humanitarianism; the second, *The Shadow on the Earth*, to the Problem of Evil; the third, *The Masterful Monk*, to the present attack on man's moral nature; the fourth, *Pageant of Life*, to the particular moral cowardice of the moment—a character study. *The Coming of the Monster* is, rather, a study of events. By sophisticates, cynics, and modernists, my interpretation of these events will be dismissed as too contemptibly simple. I am writing for such as have eyes to see, ears to hear, and minds unshackled by intelligentsia's chains.

My method, in this novel, is, in one respect, an experiment. I have deliberately adopted and adapted the Screen method for intensifying theme and incident, by the interspersion of "Interims"; cascades of events in rapid superimposition.

May I mention, to forestall doubt, that the descriptions contained in these Interims are almost wholly from actual life.

OWEN FRANCIS DUDLEY

CONTENTS

PROGNOSIS

INTERIM

INTERIM

INTERIM

Prognosis

Darkness is lifting to the dawn.

From the cross-roads the débris of a village can be seen, with roofless walls cutting jaggedly into the horizon's light, and, all around, a blackened area of tree-stumps. In the foreground there is a disused trench, against the wall of which some gassed-stiff figures are huddled stupidly, caught in a clump. From a shell-cavity, a boot protrudes entangled in a broken gun-wheel. Beyond the trench a wayside crucifix, untouched by shells, points heavenwards.

The hush, preceding the morning sounds of war, still reigns.

There is a stir, as of wings, and a whiteness is hovering above. The whiteness descends, and at the cross-roads stands an angel's blazing form. He remains motionless, gazing over the shattered village and the scene of desolation.

Above the trench the figure of Lucifer becomes discernible in dark outline, leaning with elbows on the parapet. For a while he watches the angel . . .

"God's in His Heaven; all's well with the world."

The angel disregards him. Lucifer leans forward a little: "On earth peace . . ."

He raises himself on to the parapet, using the clump of corpses; then reaches down with his hand and pulls at the heads, until a row of faces, distorted in the death-agony, are turned upwards hideously:

1

"How these Christians love one another!"...

He notices the crucifix, with the eyes of the Christus resting upon two corpses beneath His feet—the hand of one still clutching a water-bottle held to the lips of his comrade. Lucifer recoils slightly, resuming his taunts with hands together as though in prayer:

(In German) "Oh God, give us victory."

(In Russian) "Oh God, give us victory."

(In French) "Oh God, give us victory."

(In Italian) "Oh God, give us victory."

(In English) "Oh God, give us victory."

The angel has not stirred. Lucifer sighs pretentiously:

"What a problem!"

The slow whine of a shell is heard, travelling westwards. It lands on this side of the village, with sods flying and smoke rising. A travelling splinter strikes a corpse in the face, and remains embedded there. Lucifer regards the phenomenon for a moment; then pushes the face sideways with his foot:

"Turn the other cheek—you Christian!"

The face swings back.

"Little children—love one another."

He pulls away a bayonet and mimics it being driven and twisted into a body, replaces it decoratively, and folds his hands again:

"Thy kingdom come. Thy will be done on earth ... Thy kingdom come. Thy will be done ... Thy kingdom come. Thy will be done ..."

He listens, with a hand to his ear, eyes heavenwards; then studies the immobile form of the angel.

"You are like God—silent. Perhaps it is well."

He becomes confidential:

"You know what they are saying? That He is deaf? He is not there? He has failed?"

Prognosis

A second shell burst with a sharp detonation, nearer to the cross-roads. The angel has spread wide his wings, shielding the Calvary. Lucifer is interested:

"So that is why you are here."

He assumes amusement:

"Is it worth while?"

His voice is suddenly metallic and hard:

"They will not whine beneath the Cross, when this is over." *He indicates the desolation around.* "Nor cringe—in the day of revolt." *He waits. And then leans nearer:*

"Supposing men win where God has failed?"

The angel folds his wings slowly, and turns:

"Did Lucifer win—in the Day of Revolt?"

The Coming of the Monster

Chapter I

IN PETROGRAD, on a night in April, 1917, a man and woman entered the restaurant of a hotel. The few people, seated at the white-clothed tables, were talking in low, excited whispers, and glancing towards the lengths of window facing the street. Figures were passing feverishly outside, beneath a blaze of artificial light.

The man and woman looked about, chose the window side, and found a table. The woman sat down, opened a handbag and examined herself in a small mirror. She was goodlooking with the broad face of a Russian. Her eyes, however, showed an angry light, and the mirror was trembling in her hand.

The man, after giving an order to a waiter, took his place opposite, removed his cap and wiped his forehead. He was flushed, and his clothes had a disordered appearance. On his right temple there was a discoloured swelling. For a moment neither of them spoke. Then the woman released herself, barely suppressing her voice:

"You fool! Why did you do it?"

The man replied more quietly:

"I would do it again."

"You know *who* it was?"

"Yes. That is why I called him——"

5

"Called? You shouted it—'Devil!' They all heard."

"I wish there had been more, to hear."

The woman controlled herself with difficulty:

"You called *Lenin*—'Devil!'. . . *Lenin!*"

"Yes. Lenin."

She paused for words.

"Do you understand what you have done? They could have killed you on the platform."

The man fingered the lump on his forehead.

"It is fortunate that my head is hard. Oh yes, they are the men who would kill—if they ruled."

"Are you mad? Lenin's men? Do you understand—it is *Lenin* who has come back?"

"Yes. Lenin the revolutionary."

She flung back:

"Lenin will save Russia!"

"Kerensky was going to save Russia," he retorted.

The waiter interrupted them with cups of tea, which he placed on the table. The man paid him.

The woman leaned forward:

"Kerensky! A talker. An incompetent. Lenin will act. Lenin will stop the war. That was Tscheidse at the station—the Menshevik who wants the war to continue. Lenin was angry with him. Could you not see that? Fool, do you want the war to go on? Are we not sick of the war?"

"Please do not call me names," the man said. "I am not thinking of the war. Lenin is Godless."

"So much the better. We have had enough 'God'—Who does nothing for Russia. The people will be starving. This Government of imbeciles! They do nothing. There is mutiny in the Army. Soon there will be riots—against us, against the bourgeois."

The man replied firmly:

"Lenin will not save the bourgeois. He is a Marxian. His soul is steeped in Karl Marx. He will rid Russia of the bourgeois, when——"

He broke off suddenly, and listened:

"What is that?"

The woman rose, and went to the window. Figures were running past, shouting. A roar of voices could be heard, coming from a distance. The man went to the window too. The others left their tables and did the same. The woman announced:

"It is from the Nevsky Prospekt."

The roar was increasing in volume. Groups of men could be seen approaching from the Square to the right, where searchlights were playing down—the van of a dense crowd coming slowly into view. In its midst an armoured lorry was being drawn along, on which stood a solitary figure, raising his hand at intervals in acknowledgment of the ovation. A sweep of white light caught him, and stayed. The woman almost shrieked:

"It is Lenin!"

Her cry was repeated:

"Lenin!"

They watched intently. The crowd was flowing into the street where the hotel stood. As the lorry reached the corner, it halted, amidst fresh outbursts of cheering. The figure raised above the throng of heads made a gesture, and there was an abrupt silence. The woman pulled at the man's arm:

"He is going to speak!"

"The Devil is going to speak," he replied.

She hissed in exasperation:

"Keep quiet, you maniac!"

The others at the window had turned—some of them murmuring disapproval at the man's remark, the rest saying nothing. They all watched again. The figure on the lorry was standing upright, facing first in one direction, then in another, addressing the crowd. When he turned to the left, the sound of his voice carried through the windows, metallic and vibrant.

The man moved away, sat down, and lit a cigarette. The occupants of the window remained there, staring.

Another roar could be heard.

"He has ended." The woman pointed excitedly. "Look, they are moving the lorry! . . . Oh! . . . They are . . . Yes, look! look! They are coming . . . He will pass the window . . . Oh! . . ."

Outside, the front ranks of the crowd were being pressed forward, approaching down the narrow street, singing and shouting, red banners aloft, as they came. The singing prevailed as those behind took it up. It was the Song of the Revolution, the rhythm marked by the tramp of feet. It became a thunder. They were passing the windows—men and women, twenty deep, waving caps and kerchiefs. They came on and on, a surging torrent. The lorry was close. The face of the revolutionary leader could be seen. He was scanning the windows, lifting his head to the acclamations from either side, ignoring the occasional hostile shouts audible above the din.

"What a man! What a man! . . . Lenin!"

The woman had pressed against the glass. Lenin was passing the hotel. They could see him clearly now—a man with strong features and stern magnetic eyes. He was glancing at the windows of the restaurant, whose lights were catching his face.

The man, who had remained smoking at the table, all in a moment rose, approached the window, and spat. There was an angry protest at the act, mingled with isolated cries of approval. A fist was shaken at him from outside. The spittle slithered slowly down the glass. The woman pushed him away fiercely:

"Get back! . . . You savage! . . . Get back!"

The man replied with vehemence:

"I would spit in his face—the son of Satan!"

He returned to his table, and sat down with eyes gleaming.

The lorry had passed on. The mob behind was streaming by; the Song of the Revolution rising and falling. The faces at the windows opposite watched for a while, and then one by one were withdrawn. The crowd tailed off into ragged groups, the sound of the Song waning with the distance. Finally it ceased.

The woman resumed her chair, regarding him stonily:

"Are you incapable of understanding?"

"No. It is because I understand."

The entrance-doors swung open, and a group of men entered, talking boisterously. They were followed by others, women as well as men, many of them rough-looking. It became a flow into the restaurant from the street outside. The place was filling fast, everybody talking rapidly in high-pitched tones. It became a din of voices. Waiters were being called for. A commotion of bottles and glasses began.

The group of men who had first entered, had taken a table on the far side from the window, and were being served. One of them rose to his feet and tapped sharply with the edge of a plate. It arrested attention and heads turned in his direction. There was a fanatical light in his eyes. Someone shouted, "Karenov!" He acknowledged his name with a bow, and tapped again for quiet.

Then he brandished his glass:

"Comrades . . . Lenin!"

The men with him stood:

"Lenin!"

They remained with glasses raised, but not yet drinking—looking round the restaurant. Groups here and there rose to their feet with, "Lenin!" The rest looked about at each other. Some stood. The man and the woman by the window were arguing in hoarse whispers:

"Stand with me! You are my husband."

"Sit still! You are my wife."

The woman gave him a stare of defiance, rose and beckoned to a waiter. She was supplied with a glass of wine, and raised it, crying, "Lenin!" There was a silence of readiness.

The man Karenov had observed something. He was peering across the restaurant at them:

"Your husband is not so brave?"

The man called back:

"I am brave enough not to drink with revolutionaries—to their leader."

He was greeted with applause from those who were seated.

Karenov's retort rang out:

"You will not be so brave in the day of the revolution. The bourgeois will be cringing—when Lenin rules."

There was a vehement demonstration by those standing. The man flung back:

"It is easy for braggarts to talk—when they are mustered together."

There were angry shouts. Karenov had been stung:

"It will not be easy for the bourgeois to prattle—when the proletariat rules."

"Will the proletariat rule—when Lenin is in power?"

"Lenin will lead!"

"Lenin will enslave. Lenin is Godless, a Marxian. Lenin will lead against God. He will lay upon us the creed of Karl Marx. There will be no liberty, no rights. We shall be a herd of animals without souls. Our——"

"Lenin——"

The man refused interruption: "Our religion will be spat on, our churches closed. There will be no morality. You are blind! We are Christians. Shall an atheist lead us?"

A voice called:

"Better than Christ has led us!"

"Blasphemer! Have you allowed Him to lead?"

Karenov tapped violently with the plate again:

"The bourgeoi wastes his breath . . . Comrades . . ."

He waited until there was silence, then raised his glass aloft. All those standing did the same.

"Comrades, drink to Lenin! . . . Drink to the Revolution!"

"And drink to your own damnation!"

Karenov ignored him:

"I will give you the words of Lenin. Comrades, I have heard them at the station: 'Long live the Socialist World Revolution!'"

It brought a tumult of cheering. There was an abrupt silence as they drank. The woman, who had been watching, drank with them too. The man studied her doing so, in a puzzled way, as though something were being borne upon him:

"So you are no longer a Christian?"

The woman put down her glass:

"I am no longer a fool." She stared back at him defiantly: "And I am no longer your wife. I am tired of you."

He regarded her intently for a moment, oblivious of the interest aroused:

"You are unwell?"

"I was never better."

"Has Satan possessed you?"

The woman broke into harsh laughter:

"And who by the devil is Satan?"

The sally was heard throughout the room, and evoked coarse ribaldry:

"He believes in Satan!"

"The woman should have a better man!"

"It will be easy for her to find a Comrade!"

The man succeeded in singling out with his eye the last speaker—standing near the entrance. He left the woman, and made his way, unmolested, between the tables and past some waiters clustered together nervously. Near the doors he halted, and whipped round with his fist. A figure was sent crashing and sprawling amongst bottles and glasses.

The man walked out.

CHAPTER II

I N PARIS, on a night of January, 1919, a man wearing the uniform of a French poilu, stood at the corner of a *Place*, surveying the scene before him.

The great square was brilliantly illuminated. Beneath the blaze of arc lamps people were chattering, laughing, or hustling along. There were French officers in the cars streaming by. To the poilu's right *Le Grand Hôtel* with ground floor windows glowing yellow to the whiter light without, revealed its diners within. There were two smaller hotels opposite showing dancing to the public gaze. In front, on the further side of the *Place*, a church, with doors wide open, soared into the dimness of the night above. Figures were ascending the steps and entering for Benediction; through the doors, above the heads of worshippers, the choir altar was visible, glimmering with candles.

There was a grim absorption about the poilu. Except when jostled he appeared oblivious of the passers by. He was awakened, however, by a French officer suddenly confronting him. The poilu clicked his heels and saluted mechanically. The officer was scrutinising him:

"You were at Verdun. Is that not so?"

The poilu regarded him steadily, and then smiled.

"Yes, and I remember you, my officer."

The other took his hand, and held it:

"You were one of my brave men—the men who gave their word, and kept it."

He drew the poilu aside, away from the crowd:

"We will talk . . . No, do not stand to attention. We are just two men now. Forget that I am an officer."

The poilu shed his embarrassment:

"I would like to talk with you. We used to talk at Verdun. You remember?"

The officer laughed:

"I called you 'the philosopher', yes. . . . So you are not yet demobilised. But you will be, soon? Tell me—you are glad that it is all finished?"

The poilu looked doubtful:

"But, is it all finished? I have just been thinking—no, it is not all finished; they are gay too soon."

He indicated the crowd.

"How?" the other asked. "We are no longer in the trenches. We are alive. The peace-makers are assembling."

The poilu's expression was cynical:

"At Versailles, in a palace. The peace-makers will not make peace, my officer."

"And, why not? Tell me. I am interested."

The poilu unburdened himself:

"Were the peace-makers in the trenches? Do they understand? The President Wilson understands, a little. The others—no. They laugh at him, up their sleeves, at his 'fourteen points'—a dreamer! Clemenceau—no; he can see only frontiers on a map. He is a cynic: 'The President Wilson believes himself to be Jesus Christ.' M'sieur Lloyd George—he is a politician. Signor Orlando—Bah! Fireworks! General Smuts—he is a great man; an idealist—they will say yes to his face, and no behind his back . . . they have not vision; they have politics. They will bargain for peace, in the Hall of Mirrors. They will see only themselves in the Mirrors, at Versailles."

The officer was smiling, appreciatingly:

"They will not end war? I think you are right. Tell me, who will."

"The men who understand."

"And who are the men, my poilu, who understand?"

"They understand—in Russia."

The officer's eyebrows lifted:

"The Bolsheviks?"

"The Bolsheviks will end war. They will unite the workers against war, everywhere."

The officer studied him for a moment.

"But, you are not a Communist?"

The poilu shrugged his shoulders non-committally:

"There are meetings of the Communists here, in Paris. I go. They speak of what Lenin will do, when the workers rule. . . . You are astonished? But, there are French officers there, listening."

"No. I am amused. I am one of the French officers, who listen."

The poilu was plainly taken aback:

"That is so?"

The officer warned him:

"We shall agree not to report each other? I do not think we shall agree about Lenin."

The poilu recovered himself, and became earnest:

"There is truth in their speeches. They understand what is wrong; why there are wars. It is the capitalists, the politicians, the priests."

The other became earnest, too:

"A little truth, and many lies. The capitalists, the politicians? I do not know. Perhaps. It is the statesmen who make wars.

The priests—no. That is stupid, and it is malice. Lenin says 'No God, no priests; religion, it is the opium of the people.' He is stupid. Religion is here." The officer tapped his heart. "They cannot kill religion."

The poilu showed surprise:

"But, you are a Christian—a good Catholic?"

"I was not so. I am, after the war."

"And I no longer believe, after the war."

The officer regarded him.

"I shall call you the 'bad philosopher'."

"How?"

"It is bad philosophy, to hate."

The poilu looked startled.

"My friend, I have seen you, just now. You look at them dancing over there; at the profiteers and their ladies with the white arms in *Le Grand Hôtel*, drinking champagne. You say to yourself, 'How I hate them!' Am I not right?"

The other was colouring, confusedly. The officer repeated:

"I am right?"

The poilu found his tongue:

"They are swine. The dead are lying still unburied—who saved them. Do you not hate them?"

"It is useless to hate. The Bolsheviks hate."

"They are right to hate."

"No," the officer affirmed. "They will not cure the world with hatred. It is always the same—hate men, hate God. You do not believe, my poilu, because you are learning to hate. It is a bad philosophy——" He broke off, suddenly aware of being stared at by a school-girl standing on the edge of the pavement. Their eyes met, and she looked away hastily. He had an impression of flaxen hair, and curiously deep blue eyes . . . "——That is the Devil's way, and it does not make a better world. We do not change 'the swine' by hating." He noticed, as he indicated

16

the windows of *Le Grand Hôtel*, the flaxen-haired school-girl crossing the road. "I do not know politics; but I know men. And I know that it is better men who will make a better world." He touched the poilu on the shoulder: "And I know that *le bon Dieu* makes better men than the Devil."

The poilu was looking slightly uncomfortable:

"I am not yet a Bolshevik."

The open doors of the church opposite caught the officer's eye. He appeared to meditate.

"Eh?. . . You are not yet a Bolshevik? No, no, of course not. I will show you a better way."

The poilu was looking more uncomfortable:

"You are busy. I will not keep you."

"I am free. I will tell you."

The officer pointed across to the lighted doorway:

"You and I, we will go in there for the Benediction. We will——"

"But I do not believe!" came in alarm.

"Ah, you will believe in a few minutes. After the Benediction, we will find a priest, and we will make our confessions—I, because I am a wicked man; you, to make you a better man. Tomorrow morning we will make our Communions together; we will both be better men, to make a better world. And tomorrow evening we will dine together at *Le Grand Hôtel*, and drink champagne amongst 'the swine'—the French officer and the poilu! That is a good programme, is it not?"

He linked his arm in the poilu's.

"But, my officer——"

He led the dismayed poilu through the crowd in the direction of the church.

"Come on, my brave man of Verdun!"

CHAPTER III

LADY WRAY'S fingers fidgeted irritably with a curtain-sash at the window. They were fat fingers overladen with rings. The back of her ample person was turned to an overcrowded lounge, and to a girl sitting taut and upright on the arm of a divan with eyes fixed upon the beeches outside, glittering wetly along the drive. They were eyes of a curiously deep blue emphasised by flaxen hair. There was in them a look of mingled distress and determination.

The beauty of this April morning, of 1924, was lost upon them both—the vista of Kent countryside under sunshine and showers. Lady Wray swivelled round.

"Well?" came unpleasantly.

The girl transferred her gaze to a log smouldering in the fireplace, then rose and began walking about. She picked up an object from a table and put it down again.

"Can't you speak?... Verna!"

Verna, her daughter, came to a standstill:

"I've nothing more to say. I've told you, mother."

Lady Wray came nearer:

"And I've told *you!* You little fool, what do you think I've asked this crowd for?"

"I don't know. I didn't even know they were coming." Verna faced her: "They're not your friends; they're county. Why've——" She stopped short in a puzzled, apprehensive way.

"Well?"

"Mother, you've *not*——"

"Oh, yes, I have. They're coming here to—— Yes, Belton?"

A manservant had tapped and entered. Lady Wray went across. There was a whispered conversation ending with: "A dozen bottles." Belton retired.

Lady Wray resumed nasally:

"Yes, they're coming here to congratulate you—drink your health—yours and Harland's. They're coming to lunch with the pork-butchers because Harland's the son of a peer. Got it, my dear?"

Verna was staring incredulously.

"Mother, how *dare* you!"

"Come to your senses, my dear!"

The girl flared up:

"I've told you! We're *not* engaged! . . . It was private, in any case."

Lady Wray walked across to an escritoire, and came back with a letter in her hand:

"Perhaps you'll read that?"

Verna took the letter, and did so. Her fingers were trembling.

"Well?"

"Harland wrote that two days ago."

"Quite so," her mother replied. She took back the letter and read aloud: "'Verna and I are engaged. Any objections?'"

Verna informed her in a firm voice:

"I wrote to Harland last night. He knows now."

Lady Wray pondered the announcement with a slow, "Oh?"

There was an uncomfortable interval. "Oh? Really? . . . Then, you'll tell him—you were upset—unwell—anything . . . Do you see?"

"No, mother. I'm not going to be bullied into it. Harland and I are *not*——"

She stopped short. Belton had flung open the door:

"Mr. Harland Carville."

Lady Wray started. She recovered her composure sufficiently to advance with a beaming smile, and shake hands with
a tall, well-groomed person. Harland Carville crossed to where
Verna was standing. She drew away from his intention of kiss-
ing her. He assumed a look of mild surprise. His deportment,
however, remained unruffled.

Lady Wray made one or two formal remarks, glanced at
Verna uncertainly, and then excused herself and withdrew.
Harland Carville waited until the door had closed.

"What's up, Verna?"

"You'd better sit down, I think. I can tell you better."

He did so, on the divan, crossing his legs.

"Yes?"

She asked him:

"You got my letter?"

"I did. This morning. I imagine you weren't quite yourself
last night."

"I was very much myself last night."

Harland studied her. An amused smile hovered about his
lips.

"You needn't look at me like that, Harland. I'm not a child,
to be patronised."

He replied coolly:

"Do you mind explaining what all this is."

"I'm going to. Harland, I read a book of yours yesterday."

"Indeed?"

"I suppose you mean it all?"

"The book? I hope so."

"Then, I only knew you yesterday."

Harland Carville rose and walked imperturbably to the
window. He stood there looking down the drive with his

hands stuffed in his trouser pockets; then remarked without turning:

"So that's the trouble. I always thought you a bit—Victorian, Verna."

"Victorian? Because I think you're beastly?"

Harland moved round. His composure left him:

"Perhaps you'll withdraw that?"

Verna's colour had heightened:

"No, I will not. That book is you. And that book's beastly."

He managed to control himself, and light a cigarette. The match was flung into the fireplace.

"Shall we discuss this quietly?"

"There's nothing to discuss."

He inhaled deeply, and released a cloud of smoke. A hauteur was appearing:

"May I ask what you object to in my book?"

"Everything. All right, then, if you want me to—it's vile. And it's not because I'm Victorian. It's because I object to decency, and sacred things, being sneered at."

"For instance?" he asked.

"It doesn't need instances. It's the whole thing. Your whole outlook. Harland, if I'd known you were like that——"

"My dear Verna, don't get hectic. A man's a right to his own opinions."

"So has a woman, to hers."

"Certainly. Let's agree to differ, then."

Verna regarded him steadily. He flicked the ash from his cigarette.

"Oh no, Harland. It's more than differing, this. I only understood yesterday. We're poles apart, you and I. Do you realise in the least what that book made me feel? Like a knife driving into everything that's sacred to me personally. And I'm not narrow, and I'm not over-religious."

He replied emphatically:

"And do you realise in the least that I write for a purpose? And that shams are *not* sacred?"

The girl's eyes flashed:

"You might at least be honest—enough to be honest with yourself."

"What the devil do you mean?"

"Morality's another 'sham'. Isn't it? You say so. I imagine you practice what you preach?"

The colour in Harland Carville's face deepened.

"We're discussing principles."

"Yes. Have you any?"

There was an uncomfortable interval.

"Let's scrap fencing, shall we?"

"By all means . . . Harland, I'm wondering why you asked me to marry you? For a 'temporary union', or what?"

"Damn it all, Verna! A book's a book!"

The sound of crunching gravel caught their attention. A car passed the window and drove up to the portico before the front door.

"By the way, are you staying to lunch?"

He retorted sharply:

"I *came* here for lunch—not this foolery."

"Because if you are, would you mind explaining before they drink our health?"

He stared at her, then at a second car driving up outside, frowning disquietedly.

"I'm sorry, but——well, mother made a mistake."

"Look here, Verna, come to your senses!"

"I have. I informed mother just now."

There was a babel of voices in the hall, increasing every moment. The door opened, and Lady Wray entered. She glanced hastily at Verna and Harland. In the hall the insignificant figure of her husband was visible, shaking hands with people and indicating the lounge. They were calling him, "Sir William", genially. They strolled in, talking all together in level monotones, smart-looking and completely at ease. Lady Wray beamed:

"My daughter . . . You all know Harland?"

She gave him a proprietary pat on the back. Verna began shaking hands with them. Harland, after nodding recognitions and making a formal remark or two, remained silent and scowling. There was a general chatter under cover of which he succeeded in drawing aside Verna:

"Are you going to end—this farce?"

"It's ended. You read my letter."

"You mean that?"

"Most certainly I do."

Lady Wray was watching them across the room. Two more cars passed the window. Verna moved away from him and engaged in conversation with another man. A couple of voices were raising themselves above the rest:

"Colonel, you're appalling."

"I assure, my dear lady—'Men like Gods'. No clothes, no marriage."

"'If Winter comes'? Wells is leg-pulling."

"Ask Carville. We're all going to revolt. Civilised Bolshies."

"What for? I've not read it."

"Read it, my dear. We've got to damn well stick out our chests at the stars and tell the Almighty to quit. See the idea? 'Men like Gods'. Like goddesses better? What? . . . I say, Carville . . . Where's Carville? . . ."

There was a sudden lull. More people were being shown in. Lady Wray had not noticed them. She was over by the window with Harland Carville, whispering frenziedly. Harland was barely listening. She beckoned imperiously to Verna, oblivious of stares. Verna went to her, and said in a low voice:

"Mother, don't make a scene. Do you mind leaving it to me?"

Lady Wray's face took on a purplish hue. She tried to speak but her lips merely quivered. Verna said something to Harland. The hubbub of voices had ceased.

Harland, all in a moment, bowed stiffly to Lady Wray, straightened himself, and proceeded to pick a passage through the crowd.

There was an amazed silence as they made way for him. At the door Belton, entering with a tray of cocktails, stepped aside. Harland Carville passed out.

A minute later he walked swiftly past the window, down the drive.

INTERIM

Down the central thoroughfare of a Russian city a procession of young men and women is marching in broad daylight, displaying on a banner, "The Last Supper", represented as a drunken orgy.

In a law-court, under examination by a Communist prosecutor, a girl, with the face of a Madonna, is standing calm and upright. To the death sentence she replies: "I am ready. I have made my peace with God."

In a street a man, lounging against a wall, is studying the illustration, in a Moscow paper, of a Capitalist in a silk hat flogging a worker, with a Bishop in smug satisfaction looking on.

In a church an altar stands transformed into a table, behind which the bust of Karl Marx has replaced the ikon of Christ.

In a country village a mass execution is proceeding, of men and women huddled in a clump, shrieking or praying, dropping one by one before the firing squad.

In a prison-cell rats are swarming the bodies of political prisoners crushed together for warmth, some of them dying; in a corner a man is strangling himself with a strand of oakum.

On Solovetsky Island a team of political exiles are straining loaded waggons over a rough surface; on the trail behind a man lies where he has fallen. Inside a hut in the women's quarters the Camp guards are selecting for themselves from a group of female prisoners. As her name is called, one of them swings round and batters her head against the wall.

The Coming of the Monster

On an open space in Leningrad long ranks of boys and girls are at physical drill to the tune of the "Song of Freedom".

In a Communist factory in Moscow the steady hum of engines, amidst massive machinery, proclaims production and efficiency.

.   .   .   .   .

In a room in a New York Newspaper office, a man, in need of a hair-cut, is bending over the sheets of the New International, *underlining complacently sentences with a pencil: "The revolution in Russia recognises no other class but the proletariat . . . proletarian democracy annihilates tyranny . . . a new form of government must be organised by the revolutionary proletariat, as in Russia . . . the dictatorship of the proletariat . . . to promote and establish the revolution and the new society . . ."*

.   .   .   .   .

In London, a Soviet procession is moving up Oxford Street towards the Marble Arch, with lorries of children waving red flags.

Inside Hyde Park the procession has spread itself into an extensive crowd listening to a Communist orator: "Comrades, Jesus Christ, the man, is the Christ I believe in; not the Christ of Christians; not Christ, a God in Heaven. I'll take off my hat to no God in the skies. I'll take it off to Christ the working-man! Christ the Socialist! Christ the man on earth! Christ the revolutionary! And I take it off now to the Christ of today—Lenin, the world revolutionary!" He removes his hat to tumultuous cheering.

From the pulpit of a London Cathedral, on Good Friday, a Doctor of Divinity is preaching in well-modulated tones: "In these days, when educated reason revolts against dogmas to which it cannot intelligibly subscribe, the doctrine of the Redemption requires restatement in terms of modern thought, and according to the findings of modern Scriptural research. It is recognised now that Christ did not claim to be the Son of God in a physical sense such as the Gospel narratives of the Virgin Birth affirm, nor in a metaphysical sense such as is required by Nicene theology, and such as is required if we accept the mediæval conception of the Atonement. The once popular doctrine, too, of the Fall of Man being no longer tenable, we are compelled to abandon the consequent crude, I might say barbaric, notions with which Catholic theology has invested the Death on Calvary. . . ."

In char-à-bancs on the London-Southend road hot-cross buns are being consumed to the accompaniment of concertinas and mouth-organs. A child, wedged between its father and mother, tracing out the cross on its bun with an enquiring finger, is exhorted: "Nah then, aint the bun orl rite? Git on wiv it."

On Brighton promenade the Good Friday crowds are swarmed round bandstands, cars processing endlessly along the front, young men and girls making love in the shelters, queues forming outside places of amusement.

In an East-end Catholic Church, a Crucifix is laid on the sanctuary steps, with costers and dock-labourers streaming up the nave to kneel and kiss the Feet.

Chapter IV

T
HE GUIDE led them across a courtyard. It was flanked by structures representing the outside of a French château, a Mexican palace, an old-English timbered front, and on one side by a kind of long bungalow with many doors. He jerked his head in the direction:

"Stars' dressing-rooms."

They followed him behind the French château, and then between vast shapes resembling airship sheds, with "Stage 18", "Stage 19", "Stage 20", painted on immense sliding doors. Outside the postern of "Stage 21", the guide halted:

"If they're shootin', you gotta wait here."

He disappeared through the postern, which swung to after him.

The two girls regarded each other:

"Verna, it's distinctly thrilling."

Verna agreed with a nod. The guide reappeared:

"O.K. Come right in. And, say, no talkin' on the set."

They followed him through the postern. Inside, out of the brilliant Californian sunshine, it was darkness. Shapes became visible slowly; tall tripods surmounted by cylinders, with trumpets projecting; triangular towers of lattice on wheels supporting more cylinders; snaky coils of tubing curling about the floor.

"An' don't tread on the spaghetti."

They picked their way cautiously after him over the coils, and then through a maze of scenery; uncompleted architectural

31

pieces, halves of rooms, staircases finished abruptly in mid-air, clumps of artificial bushes, Kaffir huts. They crossed a Renaissance terrace, and an art bathing-pool surrounded by backgrounds strutted up from behind. Everything was dim and deserted.

Voices and bursts of music were travelling. They reached an expanse of curtain. The guide turned warningly with a finger to his lips. Round the back-cloth they came on to the set. Before them, at a distance, a concentrated blaze of arc-lamps poured down upon the figures of a man and a woman, visible between silhouettes of cameras and operators. The scene could be made out for a luxurious boudoir, uncanny-looking under green mercury lights. They were in evening dress, standing in an attitude of waiting. The cameramen, perched high behind their lenses, were listening to instructions bellowed through a megaphone by a man seated in a canvas chair. The back of the chair was marked, "Director". There were more chairs on either side of him, each marked with a name; and standards placarding in large letters, "Silence".

A sudden suspense descended.

The megaphone was directed at an invisible band, "Keep that tune under," then at the cameramen, "Cameras!" And at the boudoir, "Ready?" There was a pause.

"Go!"

The man and the woman in the boudoir sprang into life. The cameramen began winding to a passionate undercurrent of instruments. The woman was pleading in low, vibrating tones, and glancing about piteously like a trapped animal. The man in evening dress, who had abruptly transformed himself into the incarnation of leering brutality, turned, walked to a door, locked it and put the key in his pocket, returning slowly with his eyes upon the woman shrinking back in terror. He stopped and stood with his arms akimbo, laughing uglily. The woman's hand encountered an object on a table that looked like a glass-bowl with flowers. Her fingers were gripping the rim. The man saw her intention and was upon her. There was a struggle in which the bowl crashed on the floor into fragments, with the woman shrieking. The man clapped one hand over her mouth, and with the other drew out a knife. She struck at his face wildly and clawed with her nails . . . The instruments had ceased and the hiss of their breathing could be heard. . . .

A window in the left wall was opening. Through the glass a face could be seen and an arm being raised. The muzzle of a revolver intruded itself through the aperture. The man was gripping the woman's hands together, to thrust with the knife, as the explosion came. He staggered, and then jerked himself upright, staring bewilderedly. His arms relaxed, releasing the woman. She stood there swaying, as he dropped with a thud. . . .

"Cut!"

The winding of the cameramen ceased. The shot man in the boudoir assumed the perpendicular, the woman examined her face in a mirror, and the man who had fired, opened the window wide and lolled over the sill, chewing.

The Director rose from his lounging position, and sauntered across to the scene. Verna whispered to the guide: "Who are they?" He pointed to a couple of chairs on the backs of which were inscribed the names of two world-famous stars.

The Director, having engaged in an argument with the stars, returned, and, on the point of resuming his chair, noticed them standing in the semi-darkness:

"Wal, you folks? You bin nice and quiet. Come on up."

They came forward. Verna asked:

"Are we allowed to speak?"

"Sure. You can speak to me—afterwards. Sid down."

They accommodated themselves self-consciously in the canvas chairs on either side of him. The megaphone ordered:

"Get ready." Then, "Go!"

The scene was shot again. It took two minutes. Then the megaphone informed the cameramen:

"O.K. Wrap it up."

An electrician blew a whistle. The arc-lamps ceased sizzling, reddened and died out, leaving only the green glare of the mercury lamps. There was an immense fussing about, and then a hasty exodus from the place of everybody, including the stars. The Director continued to sit there, lost in thought. He jotted down something on a pad, and at length rose to find them questioning the guide.

"Say, you two'd better have lunch. D'you mind the canteen?"

Verna turned:

"That's very kind of you." She smiled at him: "You've quite forgotten me, haven't you?"

The Director called to a workman, and a light was switched on.

Verna watched his face as he examined her own, and then stretched out his hand:

"Gee, it's Miss Wray."

She took it:

"You remember?"

"I guess I got you." He dismissed the guide: "You quit, boy. I'll take 'em over." Verna slipped something into the guide's hand, and he retired.

"Yez . . . Across the pond . . . That swell house down in Kent. . . . Wasn't I doin' business with your Dad, when you come in and get me starin'?"

Verna laughed:

"That's right."

"An' I tell him—there's more business in that little gal o' yours than in all the money you're puttin' in?"

"How on earth can you remember?"

34

"Remember? I was seein' around for a gal or two like you. . . . What you doin' in Hollywood, anyway?"

"Seeing around."

"Doin' the States?"

"That's the idea." She pulled the other girl forward:

"This is Miss Terry Harcourt."

The Director shook hands:

"An' I'm right glad to meet Miss Terry Harcourt."

He regarded Verna again:

"Say, you're not married then? You're with the folks at home?"

She showed a slight embarrassment.

"Well——no, not exactly. There was a little trouble at home. We've a flat in London—Miss Harcourt and I."

"A little trouble? When was that?"

"About a year ago."

"Yum . . . Not that little proposition o' mine?"

"Oh no. Something quite different."

He shrugged, and then added:

"Ever thought o' my proposition?"

She hesitated.

"Sometimes. Not very seriously, I'm afraid."

He stood away from her.

"Gee, you're a lovely gal. . . . Say——" He went over to an arc-lamp and switched it on. A blaze of light illuminated the boudoir. He called:

"Wud you mind stannin' in that sun, Miss Wray?"

She looked at Terry Harcourt who was laughing, and then made her way amusedly towards the set:

"Why, what's the idea?"

"On the floor there, in front; an' wud you take off your hat?"

Verna did so, and took her stand where he indicated. The glare and heat were terrific. The Director, after a minute's

35

silence, told her to look up to the roof . . . then down at her feet
. . . then to the left . . . then to the right. . . .

"Nature's own colour? That hair?"

"Oh yes—absolutely."

He asked her to turn round and stand akimbo.

"An' now you're seein' somethin' in the distance, an' walkin'
towards it, wunnerin' what it is. Git me? . . . Go on."

She obeyed, until she reached the further wall of the
boudoir.

"An' now sid down on that table, smilin' an' listenin' to the
birds singin'."

She obeyed again; doing her best.

He made a sucking noise through his teeth, and disappeared from sight. A minute later a gramophone was blaring
out a dance tune. He came back shouting:

"Can you git goin' to that?"

Verna looked at him doubtfully.

"Anythin' you can do."

She jumped down, shuffled for a moment, and then broke
into a quick-step to the tune. The Director, without taking his
eyes from her, lit a cigarette and stood watching. After a while
he disappeared again and stopped the gramophone. Verna
came forward laughing and waving to Terry Harcourt. The
Director met her.

"Mr. Director, just what is all this about? I can't dance really,
you know."

He did not reply immediately, but went and switched off the
arc, came back and picked up the writing-pad from his chair.

"Miss Wray, I told your Dad, didn't I—there's money in your
little gal? Wal, there's a lot o' money in his little gal."

"Oh?"

"We cud put you through with the dancin'. I guess I cud
make a real cute thing o' you."

She was genuinely amazed.

"But—— You know nothing about me."

"Doant I? I can size up a gal same as a horse."

"Thank you!"

"I like to see them eyes o' yours flash, because you think I'm bein' impertinent. . . . Yez, violet eyes, an' a skin like milk. . . . Gee, you wudn't want the make-up man to change you." Her expression was doubtful, but he continued with his cigarette pointed at her: "An' you got wot ninety per cent o' the dolls ent got. You got personality. I'm not offendin' you; I'm tellin' you. Miss Harcourt, we'll come right along for lunch. An' after lunch—wal, I'll show you jest what I got in mind, Miss Wray. But we'll do a bit o' talkin' first."

.   .   .   .   .

An hour later, inside "Stage 20", Verna and Terry Harcourt, again on either side of the Director, were watching preparations for a shot.

Before them on the set a gorgeous construction, representing the stage of a Variety House, blazed with arc-lamps and mercury moons, the whole effect heightened by an upward glare of floor-lights. In the wings on either side of the stage a galaxy of actors, and supers, and dancing girls were stationed in readiness. From the costumes, and the lack of them, a revue was in the process of being filmed.

A whistle blew. Electricians and workmen hurried off the set. The Director turned to Verna on his right:

"The exhibition gal. Wud you mind keepin her fixed?"

Verna nodded; he had explained "exhibition" at lunch.

The megaphone blasted:

"Go!"

To a rhythm of instruments and the winding of the camera-men, four lines of dancing girls in close formation swayed into view from left and right. The rhythm increased in volume, as the lines lengthened out, four rows deep across the stage, leaving a gangway down the centre. For a while there was a steady beat of feet, until the orchestra gave the cue for a movement which placed each row in turn in front. All the girls were of the same height, their figures displayed to a maximum advantage in a minimum of covering.

The orchestra died down. A curtain in the background opened, and on a pedestal what appeared to be a statue in the nude, was revealed. The arms of the statue moved slowly upwards; the orchestra livened up into a crescendo and then into a blare of instruments as the body came to life and stepped down. It was a girl, virtually naked, her form artificially whitened. A spotlight followed her circling in and out of the dancing rows up to the footlights. The melody changed into a voluptuous, barbaric tune. She swung with the troupe into a writhing, snake-like movement, her eyes fastening upon members here and there of an imaginary audience, defying them to remove their gaze, her hands gesturing insinuatingly.

The cameramen were wheeling in for a close-up. The Director turned for a moment, to watch Verna's face.

More curtains opened up stage and two magnificent specimens of the male were standing on pedestals in the same statuesque pose. They, too, came to life, stepped down, and were followed by spotlights, gyrating in and out up to the front, and on either side of the "exhibition" girl. Like hers their bodies were artificially whitened.

The music became low and seductive, as the three of them gestured in dumb show, the men displaying their physique to the girl, hesitating between them, all the while keeping the rhythm with her feet. Her hands were seized in turn, and she was swung from one to the other. She pirouetted about them, still in doubt. They grasped for her, but she eluded them.

There was an ingenious pursuit, with each row of the troupe encircling her from her would-be captors, until finally she was entrapped, held, and raised aloft by the pair.

The deep boom of a gong intervened at the point of possession. The girl was lowered reluctantly. The three of them gained their pedestals, stepped up and, with stiffening gestures of despair, became rigid and immobile as before. . . .

"Cut!"

They waited while the Director, barely listening, dismissed a girl who had approached him outside the Stage as they emerged, with some request. She walked away slowly with her head down. He came to them:

"Wal, Miss Wray?"

Verna regarded him coolly.

"Well?"

Her manner surprised him:

"You ent lookin' pleased."

She did not reply.

"Gee, that gal wud have looked pleased." He nodded after her. "Didn' you know wot I meant—askin' you to keep that show-gal fixed?"

"I'd an idea. Yes?"

"She got the goods—personality. The're gals here wud sell their souls for the chance o' that dance. D'you git me, now?"

Verna straightened herself:

"Mr. Director, are you offering me a job?"

"I'm puttin' you a proposition. Ef you'll stay in Hollywood, I'll git you put thru' with the dancin'. An' if the Director says he got a new show-girl—wal, they got one. See? I'm reckonin' you'll pull it with the box-office."

"Oh?"

"Ef it's the dancin' you're thinkin' of, doant worry. That's trainin'. Ther a dozen gals behind her cud do that dance jest now. It's gettin' it across. An' I'm tellin' you—you cud."

"Getting what across?"

The Director appeared momentarily at a loss. He scratched his head.

"Gee, fancy a gal like you askin' that? Why, wot do the tired business men o' New York pay their money for? Acrobatics?" He laughed. "Ent you heard o' sex-appeal, Miss Wray?"

Verna was staring at him coldly. The Director began to look slightly uncomfortable. There was a disconcerting glint in the violet eyes, penetrating his languid self-assurance. He shifted a foot.

"Thank you for the lunch."

Verna turned abruptly and walked off with Terry Harcourt. The Director was left staring after them, with his hat pushed on the back of his head.

A workman in overalls emerged from Stage 20, saw him, and came up with, "Say, Director——"

"Go to b—— h——!"

Chapter V

§1

H E WAS STANDING in a doorway marked, "Stairway to Swimming-bath", looking about—a man with sharp features and humorous, watchful eyes.

The tea-tables under the awning on his left were mostly unoccupied as yet, and people still strolling the promenade deck in the afternoon sun, or lolling against the taffrail watching the Atlantic sliding away beneath—barely broken save in the liner's wake. A game of quoits was in progress through a glass screen. The voices of the players could be heard.

The man lit a cigarette, and emerged to arrange a wet bathing-suit on the taffrail. He remained there studying the shimmering waters and the haze over the horizon, until, at a sound from behind, he glanced round cautiously. Two girls were coming through the doorway, chattering cheerfully. They too, were carrying wet bathing-costumes, which they likewise proceeded to drape over the taffrail; after which they likewise remained studying the haze over the horizon.

The man himself was absorbed in the haze.

Very carefully he turned his head to find the younger of the two doing the same. They both hurriedly returned to the haze. An atmosphere of acute self-consciousness appeared to pervade all three of them. The girl suddenly began to laugh. He faced her, with a smile hesitating on his lips. The girl plunged:

"Rather silly, this? Let's introduce ourselves."

He laughed, too:

"That is a good idea. But perhaps I am a bad man."

"We've decided that you're a nice man. This is Miss Harcourt. I think you had better shake hands—it will look better. That lady is watching."

He took the cue, and also Miss Harcourt's outstretched hand. His eyes returned to the younger:

"You are Miss Wray—Miss Verna Wray?"

"And you are Captain Vivien—Captain Louis Vivien?... Yes, they're very obliging at the Bureau.... No, you mustn't shake hands with me. I'm introducing you and Miss Harcourt. The idea is that *we*'ve already met.... I think I'm doing this rather well." She looked carelessly about. "The lady in the spectacles is wondering whether I'm a vamp."

"Vamp?" he asked.

"Sorry. Of course—you're French. Vamp? A film female—an ensnarer. Miss Harcourt was a vamp before she was my staid companion."

"Verna, you're the limit!" Terry Harcourt expostulated.

Captain Vivien asked:

"Perhaps you are a—film-star. I am right?"

Verna assumed hauteur:

"No, indeed not! Is that why you wanted to talk?"

"I beg your pardon. It is the straw hair—the eyes."

"Flaxen, please. Is that why you wanted to talk?"

Captain Louis Vivien indicated the tea-tables under the awning:

"We will all have tea together, and I will tell you why. But you will promise not to vamp me? Come on."

He led the way there, ordered tea from a waiter, and invited them to sit down, with:

"I am doing this rather well. Is that not so? The lady in the spectacles is saying to herself—he is a nice kind uncle."

Chapter Five

"The lady in the spectacles," Terry announced, "is saying to herself—the niece is abnormally excited about the uncle."

"Terry, how dare you! Captain Vivien, no tea for the staid companion!"

He smiled indulgently:

"I will tell you why I have wanted to talk to you."

Verna leaned forward:

"Yes, do!"

"Because I say to myself—she wants to talk to me."

"Really! Captain Vivien!"

"Very well. It is because I have remembered you."

"*Remembered* me!"

"I have seen you in Paris, after the War. I have seen you for just one minute."

"Paris?"

"There was a French officer talking with a poilu at the corner of a *Place*, and there was a little girl with flaxen hair who was listening."

She was watching his face perplexedly.

"At night. Under a light. Opposite *Le Grand Hôtel*."

Her eyes were suddenly alight.

"You remember?" he asked.

She exclaimed:

"Yes! . . . I *do!* . . . And the French officer was arguing with the poilu about the Bolsheviks, and the little girl was wondering who they were. And the French officer turned, and their eyes met. And she looked away, blushing. . . . It was *you?* . . . Terry, this is an absolute romance!"

Terry remarked drily:

"And the lady in the spectacles is wondering why the little girl with the flaxen hair failed to recognise her uncle, in Paris."

Verna raised her voice:

"Uncle Louis! And I never knew you!" She added, sotto voce, "But this is thrilling! . . . I was a schoolgirl then—in Paris."

He proffered:

"At dinner last night I say to myself—I have seen her some-where. This morning I say to myself—it is the schoolgirl with the flaxen hair, who is now a woman."

"You remembered me? You must have been thinking about me ever since. . . . Terry, this is a super-romance."

He shrugged his shoulders:

"The schoolgirl has remembered the French officer? She has been thinking about him ever since. This is a very great romance."

"Captain Vivien!"

"That is—what do you say?—Quits! . . . Here is the tea com-ing. Yes, she is most interested—the lady in the spectacles."

§ 2

Terry was standing with a silken wrap over her arm, quiz-zing the pair of them reclined luxuriously in armchairs, with li-queurs on a table between. They were all three in evening dress.

"Terry, don't be absurd. Stay here."

She replied to Verna's invitation by draping the wrap dra-matically over her shoulders:

"I shall saunter away carelessly. As I ascend the stairs, I shall turn and look fondly at you both, and sigh, or hiccup. Exit the staid companion.

She sauntered away carelessly, with an indifferent flicking of her hands after the manner of a famous film-star, and up the stairway—to be met half-way by the lady in the spectacles coming down. They heard:

"How very fortunate! I'm longing to have a talk with you."

The lady in the spectacles was swept up again under a rapid-fire of talk. They vanished.

Captain Vivien and Verna looked at one another. They were both grinning, delightedly. He picked up their conversation from the point of interruption:

"So you did not want to be a Hollywood girl?"

"A show-girl? No."

"I am glad."

"Why are you glad?"

"I should not like to think of the schoolgirl with the flaxen hair like that."

Verna scrutinised him meditatively.

"Tell me just exactly why?"

He looked slightly embarrassed:

"It is difficult to explain to a woman. I speak English badly."

"You speak English extremely well. I want to know why."

He fingered the stem of his glass.

"A man does not respect a woman if she sells her body."

"Sells?"

"It is that, is it not? The Director says so—you dance like that, you exhibit your body, and there is money for you. Because there is always the public who will pay for women to show themselves."

There was a pause, before Verna remarked:

"Pretty beastly, isn't it?"

"I think so. Yes."

She finished her liqueur, and handed him her cigarette case. They lit up.

"Terry loathed Hollywood; although she takes it off. She calls it the Devil's Power-station. Terry likes to see the Devil everywhere. She's a Catholic." Verna asked him somewhat abruptly, "Do *you* believe in the Devil?"

"But I do. I am a Catholic."

"Oh? . . . Yes, of course, I suppose you would be."

"And I think the Devil is very clever. He understands very well the camouflage."

"How do you mean?"

"The bodies of women are beautiful; so men shall see the beautiful bodies on the screen—it is art. The marriage-bond is cruel; so they shall see free-love—it is much happier. They shall see bad things—good. You understand?"

Verna leaned back and pondered the matter.

"Yes, I think so. Captain Vivien, you're decidedly original. Do you know that?"

"Because I believe in the Devil? That is not original. It is old."

"Perhaps I'm too modern."

"The Devil also is modern."

She raised her eyebrows.

"It is modern to be—a myth." He regarded the lounge ceiling, and added:

"Uncle Louis is a strange man for a soldier; sometimes he thinks. I will tell you what I think?"

"Yes, do."

"I see much of the world, since the War—Russia, Germany, England. I come now from America. It is my work. In——"

"Your work?"

"For the Intelligence Service. In——"

"The Intelligence Service? But this is thrilling!"

"In Russia I have seen Bolshevism. And I think to myself in Russia that the Devil is very clever—they shall see my monstrosity that it is good for them; it is better for social life that there shall be no morality and no God. It shall also be better for me that I am not seen. So they shall put me on the cartoons—a myth. And the peasants, who cry that the Devil possesses Russia, shall be the uneducated fools. . . . But I—what do you say—I bore you?"

"No. I'm tremendously interested. I mean it."

"In England they laugh at the Bolsheviks—wild men with whiskers sticking out. But Bolshevism—it is not wild men with whiskers, all standing up together to shake their fists at heaven. No. First, they must have a philosophy of materialism for bad things, so that they revolt against the moral laws; because then they will revolt against *le bon Dieu* Who made the moral laws. That is the Devil's way."

She asked him:

"Is that what's happening in Russia?"

"It is also happening everywhere. It is happening in England."

"Is it?"

"I think so."

She considered.

"Morals are pretty putrid at present, I suppose."

"Because the Devil laughs—we will have civilised Bolshevism for civilised people."

"I'm not quite sure what you mean by that."

"Moral restraint, it makes inhibitions—so we will have moral freedom; there are too many people—we will have birth-prevention; clothes, they are bad for the health—so we will have nudism. We will have a healthier and a happier world."

Verna crushed out her cigarette end and said:

"Um."

She remained silent for a moment.

"We've gone from Hollywood to the Devil." Her eyes considered him. "Some people would call you narrow. . . . You're in the Intelligence Service?"

"I will be narrow, then."

He was not to be drawn on the Intelligence Service.

Verna smoothed her dress over her knees. She looked up, hesitatingly. He was drumming with his fingers on the table.

"Captain Vivien, I'd like to tell you something."

"Tell me."

"Last year I became engaged to somebody. It was a very short engagement. It lasted about forty-eight hours. I needn't go into details; but I happened to read a book of his the day after I had promised to marry him. He's a writer. Does this interest you?"

"Very much. Uncle Louis likes romances."

"It wasn't a romance. My people were desperately keen on it, because he was the son of a peer. When I read his book I almost hated him."

"It was not a nice book? No?"

"It was the sort of book that takes everything sacred and beautiful out of human life—one long sneer. I hadn't imagined him capable of writing it. I told him he was beastly."

Captain Vivien smiled:

"Some people would call you narrow. Yes?... And so you did not marry him?"

"I did not. That's why I'm with Terry in London now. My mother—— Things became impossible at home, after it."

He asked:

"And why have you told me?"

"I suppose because there's something sympathetic about you, and I want you to tell me I was right. It left me rather bitter, with everybody calling me a fool. We're estranged completely—my people and I."

Captain Vivien lit another cigarette, thoughtfully.

"You are an idealist? Is that not so?"

"I suppose I am. Yes."

"Then I am glad you did not marry Harland Carville; you would not have been happy."

Verna sat bolt upright.

"But you have given me the clue. It is a habit of the Intelligence Service. . . . We have been very serious; we will have more Hollywood now." He directed her attention to the stairway. She hastily recovered herself.

Terry was descending in another role, with mannerisms recognisable for those of a Hollywood star "crook"; gaining the floor with catlike tread and narrowed eyes.

"Hist! . . . Ve are alone?"

Verna roused herself and played up to her, gliding snakily on to the imaginary set. The "crook" held a spectacle-case for a revolver. Their eyes met in ominous silence. Verna tapped the revolver with her finger-nail significantly.

"You haf——?"

The "crook" nodded slowly, oozing with infinite cunning.

They both nodded and oozed. The tips of Verna's fingers rubbed together purringly:

"It ees good. Verra good."

"Zee gods haf decreed."

They raised their eyes piously. Verna's fell slantingly on the "crook's" person:

"Vere ees blod on you."

The "crook" spread her hands indifferently:

"It ees noddin. A leedle spurt. I shoot her in zee spectacles."

A voice came from the top of the stairs:

"Miss Harcourt! . . . Miss Harcourt!"

There was a skelter, and next moment they were both sitting, engaged in quiet conversation with Captain Vivien. The lady of the spectacles appeared, descending the stairway, peering and blinking in the direction of their corner.

"Miss Harcourt?"

Terry turned:

"Oh, I'm so sorry. . . . Yes, of course, you gave me them to hold."

She produced the spectacles apologetically.

§ 3

The night was warm, and its stillness undisturbed save by the band's melody from the ball-room below, where a fancy-dress riot was in progress. It was the last night of the liner's passage from New York.

They had been dancing down there, and were now watching from the top deck the pathway of the moon across the ocean—Captain Vivien rigged up as a swashbuckler with a fierce moustache and a pair of wooden pistols in his belt. Verna was a Columbine. Nearby a man in evening clothes was pacing up and down, his figure showing portly in the moonlight. There was an extreme impatience in his manner. Verna had already glanced round, and seen him eyeing Captain Vivien's back.

"I've an idea that this person behind wants to talk to you."

Captain Vivien replied without looking round:

"I also have an idea that Mr. Henry Meyer wants to talk to me. He is fat with a bald head—is that not so?"

"How on earth——"

"It is a habit of the Intelligence Service. Yes, Mr. Henry Meyer has a lot of things which he wants to say to me; so I have found a lot of things to say to him. Perhaps you will not care to listen to two men saying rude things——"

"Oh, I'd love it."

"It will be better that you go."

"I'm going to be absorbed in the moonlight on the waters."

"You are an obstinate young lady."

The Columbine moved away, and leaned over the taffrail further along, apparently engrossed in the beauty of the night. The swashbuckler sauntered in the other direction. The portly person came to a standstill, cleared his throat, and approached with his shirt-front popping ominously:

"You are free, sir?"

Captain Vivien faced him:

"Indeed, yes. Good evening. I take off my moustache to you."

He unclipped it from his nose.

"Are you aware, sir, that I've been wasting a large part of the day trying to get hold of you?"

Captain Vivien smiled pleasantly:

"I have noticed it. Yes?"

The portly person raised his voice:

"And that there are people on this boat who object strongly to certain remarks of yours in the smoking-room last night?"

Captain Vivien smiled more pleasantly:

"You interest me. You will have a cigar?"

The portly person waved aside the proffered cigar-case and continued more loudly:

"And that I, for one, took them as a personal affront?"

Captain Vivien suggested:

"You will like a loud-speaker?"

The portly person contained himself with an effort.

"I am not two thousand people whom you address. We will talk more quietly—Mr. Henry Meyer?"

He started perceptibly.

"My name is Harding."

Captain Vivien said in a low voice:

"But I think Mr. Harding was the Mr. Henry Meyer of the Californian Oil Syndicate. Perhaps he has forgotten? And the employees to whom he has paid a slave-wage and who were defrauded? And the strike? And the riots in Angel City where they have made the name of Mr. Henry Meyer—stink, because he pays the newspaper to say it was Bolshevism? So Mr. Henry Meyer thinks it is better to change his name that stinks; and now he is Mr. Harding, business-man of New York City?... You will pardon me? It is a habit."

Captain Vivien lit a cigar unhurriedly, without removing his eyes from the other—dumbstruck for a reply. From behind it he added:

"But it is not my business. I mention it; that is all. Because Mr. Harding who is so honourable, says that I offer him a personal affront last night. No, I shall not mention it about Mr. Henry Meyer to your friends, who object strongly to what I have said, and who wait now in the smoking-room downstairs for Mr. Harding to come and tell them, 'I have made this impertinent Captain Vivien apologise'."

"What the devil——"

"It is a habit." Captain Vivien waved his hand self-depreciatingly. "But Mr. Harding is careless to talk to his friends on the promenade deck while Captain Vivien is above, watching the beautiful moonlight on the waters."

"You damned eavesdropper!"

"It is not good for Mr. Harding to be excited. He has high blood-pressure perhaps? It will be better if he returns quietly to his friends in the smoking-room and tells them—this impertinent Captain Vivien has no apology to offer. You will listen, please. He has not intended a personal affront to Mr. Harding, Mr. Goldstein, Mr. Samuel, Mr. Maynard, and the big money-men of New York who cross to England on this boat. He has expressed his opinions about the magnates of commerce in general, as also the argument was general. If—what do you say?—If the cap fits—— You are going? . . . I wish you goodnight."

The portly person achieved an expletive, wheeled round abruptly and made off towards the cabins. Captain Vivien was suddenly in front of him, with a wooden pistol pressed against his expanse of stomach:

"No. That is the way, down there—to your friends."

The portly person spluttered incoherently, reversed, and found the stairway. Captain Vivien watched him disappear, replaced the pistol in his belt, and resumed his moustache. He drew slowly from his cigar, his eyes still on the stairway; then turned to find Verna at his side.

"Captain Vivien, you're priceless!"

"You have been absorbed in the moonlight on the waters?"

"Absolutely. I missed something about an Oil Syndicate."

"I did not wish that you should hear it."

His tone surprised her.

"Are you annoyed with me? For listening?"

Captain Vivien studied her. Their eyes met. Her own dropped suddenly.

"It would be difficult to be annoyed with you for a long time . . . *Petite enfant!*"

"Great uncle!"

"You are very beautiful tonight."

The Columbine curtsied, and asked hastily:

"Please, will you tell me what happened? Last night?"

"It is time for all good children to be in bed."

"Please."

"It will not interest you."

The Columbine's foot stamped:

"It *will*."

Captain Vivien laughed.

"Nice uncle."

He contemplated the ocean for a moment.

"I do not know in the smoking-room that Mr. Harding is Mr. Henry Meyer; and I do not know that Mr. Goldstein, Mr. Samuel, Mr. Maynard and the big money-men of New York are there, with the men who are talking, because I do not know their faces. I do not begin it; I am asked whether I consider Bolshevism—will it capture the world? And I say that it is the money-men, and the big men of the Press, and the Movie-magnates, and the dirty-show Producers, and the irreligionists and immoralists, who should know. They ask me to explain myself; so I say—because they make injustices and cruelties and lusts and hatreds; they make the ugly world which breeds Bolshevism. I do not know then that I talk to a millionaire, to a newspaper man, to a film-magnate, and to men who are in the show-world."

"This is splendid!"

"I know only that they are immoralists and irreligionists because they make the smoking-room into a cesspool with their talk, while I am reading the newspaper. It is Mr. Goldstein, I think, who is angry first and who says I talk through my hat, and Mr. Samuel who says I have the anti-Capitalism bee in my bonnet; so I explain that I do not have a hat and a bonnet also, and that I do not refer to Capitalism, but to the money-men who have no justice, and who crush the workers and make them Communists. I think it is Mr. Maynard who says that the Press and the amusement-providers give the public only what they want, and I agree that sewers are for sewage, which he does not like; so I say that I do not refer to the good newspapers and shows. '*Good*, be damned!' He does not like me at all—I am a moralist; morality, it is all so much convention: 'Dance 'em naked, if the public want it!'"

Captain Vivien smiled to himself.

"I ask him—do his sisters dance like that? He thinks I am rude—my opinion was asked about Bolshevism. I say I can understand it is distasteful, about his sisters. When he has exploded, I tell them all that I have introduced these matters because they ask me—do I consider Bolshevism will capture the world? And I consider it is a question for the money-gods and irreligionists and immoralists who make the way for Bolshevism, to decide. They answer that Bolshevism is economics, and wish that I leave out religion and morals which are not for the smoking-room. I say that I had observed so, for which I am very unpopular, and Mr. Harding says that I insult them."

Captain Vivien paused and flicked the ash from his cigar. "Some ladies, who are too much painted, come into the smoking-room while I am still very unpopular, and they are impatient for the men to come along. So I apologise for detaining them from their wives, and the painted ladies snigger, but the men are most embarrassed. So I apologise to the ladies for the mistake. Then I walk out. That is what has happened last night. . . . You are satisfied?"

She was laughing.

"And now I apologise to you also."

She stopped, surprised.

"For what?"

"Because they are not nice to talk about, and I have wanted this last evening to be pleasant."

"But you're being most amusing."

There was an abrupt silence between them. She looked away from him, over the shimmering waters, suddenly self-conscious.

Captain Vivien drew a little nearer.

"The last night of the great romance."

"Of the French officer and the schoolgirl with the straw hair," she supplemented without turning.

"Of the Uncle and the niece."

"Of the swashbuckler and the Columbine."

"Of the lady in the spectacles," came from behind them. They started. It was Terry at the top of the companion-way, arrayed in a College hat and gown with an immense pair of spectacles on her nose. A clown in a long hat was following unsteadily up the stairs: "Sorry, Miss Harcourt. Damned sorry! No offence meant. . . . Come down!"

Terry ignored him and greeted Captain Vivien:

"I take off my spectacles to you!"

"I take off my moustache to you!"

They removed and replaced their respective decorations. The clown called:

"I take off my hat to you! . . . Come on down!"

Captain Vivien advanced to the top of the companion-way and examined him:

"I take off my pistols to you!"

The clown found two wooden pistols barring his way, and lost his sense of humour:

"What the devil d' think you're doing?"

He tried to push past and reach Terry, but suddenly found himself in a grip of steel.

"You are drunk. I take off your hat for you."

Captain Vivien did so and threw it down the stairway:

"You will follow your hat, and not Miss Harcourt."

For a moment the clown looked dangerous.

"You will follow your hat?"

He hesitated; then decided that discretion was the better part of valour. His humour returned. He felt Captain Vivien's biceps admiringly, and patted his cheek. Captain Vivien smiled: "You will have a little keepsake?" He handed him his moustache. The clown clipped it on at an angle under his nose, descended carefully and with supreme dignity, came up again with his hat on, raised it, and again descended. There was a crash below followed by a generous flow of adjectives. They watched him pick himself up and move off, singing.

Terry said, "Thank you," to Captain Vivien. "I am the bold, bad swashbuckler, tonight," he replied. She put in, "Whom the Columbine vamped by pale moonlight." "While the Girton Girl was getting tight," from Verna.

She asked:

"What have you been doing?"

Terry answered:

"Unhooking that clown, dancing, and visiting the sick," and then abruptly asked Captain Vivien a completely irrelevant question:

"Have you ever been to Lourdes?"

His forehead wrinkled:

"To Lourdes?... Why, yes I have been to Lourdes."

"Because," she informed him, "there's rather an interesting person on board."

He smiled:

"The young man with the old man's face, who stoops, and who is watching the dancing in the ball-room when the Girton Girl speaks to him?"

She raised her eyebrows:

"Is there anything you don't observe?"

"It is a habit of the Intelligence Service," said Verna.

"Tell me," he requested.

Terry did so:

"He's ill, desperately. They've given him two years—to live. I told him I was a Catholic. He wants to go to Lourdes."

"Yes?"

"He's rather strange about it. Sort of defying the Almighty to put him right. Damnably unjust, and all that."

Captain Vivien mused for a moment.

"But he wants to go to Lourdes? And you would like—that I talk with him? That is what you mean?"

"Yes. . . . Will you?"

"Indeed, we will talk—tomorrow morning."

She pressed his hand gratefully, and then peered down the companion-way:

"All clear! Cheerio."

"Moustachio!"

The Girton Girl vanished with a wave down the stairs. They

were alone again. Captain Vivien pointed to a couple of chairs. They strolled slowly across the deck and occupied them. Verna murmured:

"Are we going to dance again?"

"It does not look like it, because we sit down. . . . Also, I have said—it is the last night of the great romance."

She asked quickly:

"Captain Vivien, what is Lourdes exactly?"

He examined the cigar stump in his fingers. "That clown has broken my cigar." He flung it away and lit a cigarette.

"Do you mind enlightening a heretic?"

He meditated.

"Lourdes? It is an experience."

She looked up.

"It is something which happens there. But one must go to Lourdes to know that it is true."

"Oh? . . . The're supposed to be miracles? That's why he wants to go?"

"The young man with the old face? Perhaps he says, I will go to Lourdes to find out if the Almighty God can cure me. But perhaps the Almighty God says—No, I will do something better. I will take from him his despair; I will give him something to live for and something to die for. Oh yes, there are miracles—at Lourdes."

He crushed out his cigarette under his foot, and then watched her profile in the moonlight.

"Perhaps one day you will go there. It is what Immaculate Mary has said—they must come."

The profile did not move.

"I'm hopelessly worldly, you know."

He disagreed:

"But you have very great ideals."

"Have I?"

"You do not marry Mr. Harland Carville, and you do not become a Hollywood show-girl."

She said nothing. Her face was still averted.

"I think you are different from what you look like."

"A film-star. Thank you."

"I express myself badly; you are very good—inside yourself."

"Am I? . . . Anyway . . ."

There was an interval.

"Anyway . . . It is the last night——"

"Of the great romance. Give it a rest, Uncle."

"You do not like me to say so?"

She did not reply.

"It is because I want you to say— No, it shall not be the last time that we see one another."

"The Intelligence Service is not very acute."

He avowed:

"I am shy. I require much encouragement. And, you and I, we have not been properly introduced."

"Rather too late now, isn't it?"

Their eyes met. Verna suddenly laughed.

"What sort of encouragement do you want?"

"I would like that my niece gives me the address where she and Terry live in London."

"Why?"

"So that some time when I am in England the great romance shall continue."

Verna assumed a doubtful expression:

"This is not a habit of the Intelligence Service?"

"It is my first great romance."

She took his outstretched hand:

"All right . . . This is my first great vamp."

He smiled:

"The great romance, it is not finished."

CHAPTER VI

THE MONK made a correction; then gathered up the sheets in order and clipped them together. He took a large envelope from a drawer of the writing-table, addressed it to the editor of an English newspaper, leaned back and contemplated the range of Alpine heights through the square of the window. The light from the same revealed a barely furnished cell. The monks of Issano asked little of this world, perched on a bleak bastion of rock beneath the eternal white. There were English books and papers about him, and there was an unmistakably English look about Fra Anselmo himself—in the steady grey eyes and strongly chiselled features and whole powerful build of his person.

His eyes returned to the manuscript. It was headed, "The Tide of Revolt". He picked it up, revealing, in doing so, the middle finger of his right hand missing. Having jerked back the sleeves of his habit, he turned over the first two pages and began to reread what he had written:—

". . . The Wellsian revolt is fundamentally the revolt of Bolshevism. In the Utopia of Mr. Wells' envisioning all 'the lies of dogmatic religion and dogmatic morality' have been flung aside. The marriage-bond is a thing of the past. Free-love reigns supreme. Stark Apollos wander about in Olympian nakedness, marvels of grace and physical splendour. These nudists, the final product of the 'Great Revolution that is afoot on earth', have taken hold, soul and body, of the life and destiny of the race. They 'laugh at the things they had feared' and 'lift their daring to the stars'.

"That is the Wellsian vision of the new—or rather, nude—order replacing the order of Christian civilisation, and representing the imagined fulfilment of Humanitarian hopes.

"May we remark, *en passant*, that these gods and goddesses solemnly strutting about their Wonderland, doing their tremendous work of making everything and everybody fit and beautiful, strike us as irresistibly funny. What precisely is this immense hubbub all about? The Christian order has at least a very definite and final goal ahead. Their creator takes his naked Utopians as seriously as they take themselves. They are all that is noble and pure—now that morality has been abolished. It must be very wonderful to be like that. . . .

"Present day Nudists, now given a capital N, are likewise advocating the 'back to nature' policy for the attainment of human perfection, although, so far they have failed to follow nature; animals have at least the decency to go about on all fours. . . .

"We incline to think that Nudists fail to study sufficiently the psychology of nudism. There is nothing very original about the cult; the practice of undressing is common in asylums, with the violent type. Nudism is an abnormality—an act of violence. The Utopians are quite consistent in defiantly exhibiting their bodies, and gesturing their revolt—to signify a world gone violently mad. They are consistent too in taking themselves so seriously; it is a habit of the unbalanced. That Nudists are not regarded as certifiable is due to the irrationality of the age of which they are the product.

"In Utopia Mr. Wells has merely advanced that irrationality to its logical conclusion—the replacement of the rational by the irrational, of God by Man, of morality by licence. For the climax of irrationality is man's disclaimer of his first rational act, the acknowledgment of His Creator and the recognition of His moral laws.

"However, we are concerned with something bigger than a cult. We have instanced it as symptomatic of these days. . . . The 'Great Revolution that is afoot on earth' at least is not a fantasy. The tide of open revolt against religion and morality is even now sweeping the civilised world and threatening the whole Christian order of life. Bolshevism is but the Russian expression of what in Europe and America is less readily recognised, or perhaps less readily admitted. Modernism, Divorce, Birth-prevention, the post-war maelstrom of pagan pleasure are equally a revolt against Christianity, the marriage-bond, the moral law and the supernatural. This desperate anxiety for ape ancestry is merely man's revolt against his own human nature and moral responsibility.

"It might not be favourable to Western self-esteem; but were this morally soft generation to refrain from calling retrogression 'progress', paganism 'culture', licence 'freedom', it would at least be honest with itself. Until then there can be little hope of a return to that moral stability which is the one bulwark of civilisation.

"The writer sees two international forces of consequence in the world today: the Papacy with Catholic solidarity behind, standing for a Divine order, and law on earth; and the 'Great Revolution that is afoot' against all that Catholicism upholds. Between the two the issues lie.

"Between the two, ultimately, men must decide—for the life or death of a whole world's soul.

"ANSELM THORNTON."

The monk folded the manuscript, and was placing it in the envelope he had addressed as the tap came on the door. He called, *"Avanti."* A lay-brother appeared, spoke to him in Italian, and retired.

Chapter Six

He laid the envelope on the table, rose, and went out and down a corridor to a door on the other side which was open. A voice invited him in. He entered, closing the door behind him. At a writing-desk the Abbot was seated with an open letter in his hand. He indicated a chair, and the monk sat down. The Abbot, a lean man with a hooked nose, stroked his chin pensively before saying in Italian:

"Well, what am I to do, Padre Anselmo?"

The monk replied, in the same language:

"How, Father Abbot?"

The Abbot handed him the letter. The monk read it through slowly. Their eyes met as he returned it.

"You have expected this?"

The monk smiled non-committally.

"Last time," the Abbot informed him, "you came back without a finger; this time you will come back without a leg or an arm?"

"I will try to keep my head," the monk answered.

The Abbot assumed severity:

"But I have not yet said yes. Perhaps I shall say, no—this monk of mine makes trouble when he goes to England. He will be locked up."

"St. Peter was locked up, Father Abbot."

"There will be no angel sent to release Padre Anselmo."

The Abbot drummed with his fingers on the desk before him. He consulted the letter.

"For a year? . . . And then it will be for another year. He is tenacious, the Abbot in London. It is a bad habit of Abbots."

"It is a good habit of Abbots to let go?"

The Abbot smiled at the sally:

"My Anselmo, you wish me to believe that you will be glad to go to England, because already you know that I shall say to you, go. But your heart is in Issano."

The strong lines of the monk's face relaxed.

"Issano is my home."

"The heart is where the memories are."

"I meant my spiritual home, Father Abbot."

"I understand. But we are human."

He leaned forward and laid his hand on the monk's knee:

"You will have memories always of things which have happened at Issano, things of which you do not speak, because they are sacred—two men who came, and went away to die, both in their own way for God. I have thought always that they have learned at Issano—to die like that."*

The monk's eyes were resting on the hand.

"In the chapel of the Crucifix of Limpias you remember always Captain Rodney, and in the Church, beneath the Cross you see always a cripple lying there. Your heart is here in Issano. And yet I say to you, go to England, because I believe it is from God; you have not asked to go."

The monk looked up.

"For how long, Father Abbot?"

"I cannot say to you. They will ask of you much work, as before. But you are still young, and you are strong; you will like the speaking and the preaching—and the adventures. . . . You smile. It is true. You are always the adventurer, Padre Anselmo."

The monk assumed astonishment.

"But you are a good adventurer, for God; and I do not think the Devil likes you. You shall go and spoil his work in England. . . . Now."

The monk rose, genuflected, and kissed the Abbot's ring. He remained on one knee while the Abbot blessed him, and then laid both his hands on his shoulders.

---

* Referring to incidents in "The Masterful Monk" and "Pageant of Life."

Chapter VII

§1

THE ONLY LIGHT was from two miner's lamps casting pale circles on the blackness of the tunnel wall, and revealing in vague outline the figures of the man and woman carrying them and groping carefully along. It was uncannily silent, save for the occasional tap of picks coming cavernously from somewhere ahead.

Verna's voice said:

"It's weird, this."

The man in front asked:

"How do you like it?"

"A bit warm. How far are we down?"

"This seam? About half a mile—below Yorkshire."

"Oh? One doesn't want to think too much."

He said:

"A man I brought down last year started thinking. Got a touch of claustrophobia. We had to hold him down——"

"Thank you, Jim. Do you mind going on? I want to see them picking."

They continued their groping along, stooping now. The roof of the seam had lowered.

"You're a plucky kid, Verna."

"I'm not a kid; I'm twenty-three, and I'll look fifty if we ever get back to daylight."

"You'll look entirely black." He held his lamp in front to

guide her feet.

"Coal-dust's good for the complexion?" she asked.

"Excellent. If it's your own."

"The coal-dust is the Company's, Mr. Manager?"

"Clever little cousin!"

He stopped, and linked his arm in hers, ostensibly to keep her from stumbling.

"Jim, it's easier if you go on in front." She unlinked the arm. He led on ahead, with, "You're not very cousinly." They reached a bend in the tunnel. The sound of picks had become louder. Round the corner there was a sudden access of light. Jim cautioned her to mind her head; for the roof had lowered again and the sides narrowed in. They crouched their way along. The heat was become stifling.

"What's that sound?"

"Compressed air," he told her.

"Oh?"

They came to some lamps standing on the floor of the seam. Jim ordered, "Stay here a moment."

He went on. Verna remained there, peering ahead. She could make out the ceiling of the seam shored up with timbers and, through a haze of coal-dust, the shining white bodies of men streaming with sweat and streaked with black. They were wearing grimy shorts. Some were sitting as they picked, others on one knee. There were occasional wrenching sounds and dull thuds. Jim was speaking to one of the men, apparently finding fault with something. The others were listening as they worked:

"All right, Verna."

She scrambled along and reached him. The miner to whom he had been speaking, turned and had a look at her:

"Ardoo, Miss?"

Verna smiled at a black face.

"Arwudger like this job?"

"I'd rather like to try. May I?"

"Do a bit o' pickin'?... 'Ere!... Get thaar, Miss."

Jim's voice came unpleasingly:

"I wouldn't, Verna. You'll damage yourself."

The miner ignored him:

"Ar won't let yer come t'arm, Miss." He moved aside for her to take his place. "On yer knee, like me mate thaar." She obeyed, and he handed her his pickaxe. "Yer see that chink? Yer just 'it it."

Verna steadied herself, and struck.

"'Ave anuvver."

She struck again.

"Nar!"

The third one did it, and a heavy chunk of coal dropped with a thud. The miner spat.

"Yer've done it slick." He grinned: "Goin' ter take it 'ome with yer?" The other men had turned to watch. Verna looked up at Jim: "Not bad, that?" He did not reply, but shouted suddenly:

"Now then, get on with it there!"

Verna stared at him. The miner made a grunting noise. They resumed their work, a couple of them muttering audibly.

"Come on, Verna."

She stretched out her hand to the miner: "Well, goodbye—mate. Thanks very much." He grinned and took it: "Gow!... you're all raht."

"Come on, Verna."

He motioned in the direction of the lamps. She regarded him for a moment, and then made her way back until she reached the bend. There she turned and watched. Jim had moved up to the two men who were muttering. She heard:

"I'll have none of your damned insolence."

They appeared to take no notice.

"Do you hear—you two?"

One of them answered:

"Ay, ar can 'ear."

"Well, keep your tongues to yourselves, next time."

The other man's head turned:

"Gow ter 'ell."

There was a petrified silence. Then:

"Oh?... You know who I am? The manager?"

"O ay, ar knows." The voice was raised. "An' ar knows wot's goin' t' appen t' yer afore long—an' the likes of yer. . . . Ay, it's yore sort——"

"Stow that!"

An oath came.

"When's your next shift?"

"Yer can find that owt for yer b—— self."

Jim succeeded in keeping himself in hand. He hesitated, turned, and made his way up the seam. Past the lamps he called:

"You'll find your instructions at the pithead. And don't come whining——"

Another oath cut him off.

§ 2

In the engine-room at the pithead, half an hour later, Verna, still in her overalls, her face streaked with black, was listening indifferently to Jim explaining the mechanism. A vast piece of machinery was in motion, controlled from above by a solitary engineer, who had just pulled a lever, revolving the giant wheel.

"That runs the cable to the shaft-head. If you—— This isn't interesting you?"

"I'm not in the mood. I'll get these things off, I think, and wash."

"You're still peeved?"

"It's not a question of being peeved," she answered. "I've told you what I think."

"My dear Verna, that sort of thing's not allowed in the pit. Morrison's a foul-mouthed Communist. Lord, do you imagine there's a manager in England who'd keep on a man after a thing like that?"

She replied emphatically:

"Yes, I do—if it was the manager's fault. You got his wool out."

"Because I told them to get on with it?"

"No, your way of treating them—like dirt."

The wheel had stopped revolving, and there was a cessation of noise. Jim lowered his voice:

"Do you mind listening? I can tell you this; something's going to happen, unless the men are kept in hand. That wasn't bluff of Morrison's. Perhaps you don't appreciate what a strike——"

"Oh, heavens! If you *won't* see! . . . I'm not talking about discipline. I'm talking about bullying——"

"And I'm talking about rank Red Communism," he retorted. "That type doesn't understand politeness. They're run by agitators—paid, Bolshevik agitators out for a general strike. Morrison's one of those skunks who'll go round——"

"I've heard all that," she cut him off. "You're only assuming. He was up against 'your sort'."

"Lord, is it any good arguing? Let's drop this."

Verna regarded him for a moment:

"No, I don't think it's any good arguing at all. I'll go and change."

She walked towards a door on the right. Jim followed:

"I say Verna, look here."

She turned:

"Yes?"

"You're not going to let this spoil things?"

"What things?" she asked.

"Well . . . we were getting on so damned well."

"Really? Were we?"

Jim stood there, biting his lip.

"Damn it, you're not over encouraging."

"And you're not over tactful."

Jim planted himself between her and the door. There was a sudden light of passion in his eyes:

"Look here, Verna——"

"That man up there's watching. Please open the door, Jim."

"I want to say something."

"I think you'd better not."

"Why?"

"Well, if you want to know——"

The door swung open and a man entered hurriedly. Jim recovered himself, and regarded him with annoyance:

"Yes? What is it?"

Verna moved away. The man seemed agitated. He said something to Jim in an undertone. Jim muttered, "Oh?" and informed her:

"I say Verna, there's been some darned accident in the pit."

Verna came back:

"Accident? . . . What, one of the men?"

The man touched his cap:

"Chap called Morrison, Miss."

Verna started. Jim said:

"You get changed, Verna. I'll not be long."

She ignored him, and enquired of the man:

"What's happened to Morrison?"

"Dunno yet, Miss."

Jim gave him an order, to which he replied:

"Ther afraid to move 'im, sir."

He was commanded testily:

"Then, get a call through to the M.O.—to go down."

"Ar've done that, an' ar carnt 'ear nowt. T'doctor's some-whaar away."

Jim exclaimed, "Lord! . . ."

His attention was suddenly directed to the engineer above taking a phone call with, "Righto, mate," and then pulling a lever. The wheel began to revolve on the reverse. He shouted:

"Who the devil's that going down?"

The engineer called that he would ask. They waited until the cage had dropped. The engineer phoned his enquiry, and remained listening. Jim was told:

"Doctor, sir."

"The M.O.?"

"No, sir—a doctor as was passin' by t'pithead. 'E offered to go down."

The information puzzled him. Jim remained still for a moment; then shrugged his shoulders:

"Come on, Verna."

They followed him through the door.

§ 3

Verna reached the pithead from the changing-room as the cage was being signalled, coming up. She had removed her overalls and washed. Near the shaft-frame, outside the office Jim was pacing about.

The shaft-wheel slowed down to a standstill, and next minute four men emerged from the frame with a stretcher on which a figure lay. They looked about. Jim advanced to meet them. Verna heard: "Where's the doctor?"

They lowered the stretcher until its uprights rested on the ground. The biggest of the four came forward. He was wearing a clerical collar streaked with black from the pit, like his face:

"I'm the doctor, for the moment."

Jim studied him uncomprehendingly.

"Only qualified medical men are allowed down the pit." He added, "In a case of this kind," and indicated the stretcher.

"I happen to be one."

It put Jim at a loss for a moment.

"Oh?... Well, I'll take your word for it, sir."

He walked across and took a look at the figure on the stretcher. Verna made a move nearer. Jim saw her coming and met her half way:

"Better wait at the car, Verna. He's not a particularly pleasant sight. I'll be along when the ambulance comes."

"I'd rather stay here, if I'm allowed to. Is he very bad?"

Jim involuntarily glanced towards the big man, who came up and informed them:

"I'm afraid so. Legs crushed."

A pair of steady grey eyes met Verna's, and then turned to Jim:

"Will that ambulance be long?"

"Any time now."

"Because it's a case for immediate amputation. I suppose that car——?"

The big man nodded towards the road. Jim remarked shortly:

"That car's mine. I'm using it."

The other said, "Naturally," and turned his back on him to ask Verna, "I think you must be—— Morrison wants to speak to you, I think."

Verna followed him to the stretcher, and looked. Morrison was lying on his back with a blanket over the lower part of his body. There was bandaging round his head, stained with blood. He was not unconscious, for his lips were twisting in pain. The big man watched him for a moment and then moved away. Verna asked one of the bearers in an undertone:

"How did it happen?"

"Beam broke, Miss. Got a fall on 'im."

Morrison evidently heard, for his eyes opened and he looked up. Verna dropped on to her knees at his side.

"I'm so sorry."

Morrison stared.

"Yer the young leddy—as wor down thaar?"

Verna nodded.

"Ar wor thinkin'——Ar wor thinkin' just afore t'appened, as 'ow yer muster 'eard me." He screwed his head round painfully: "The boss aint 'ere?"

"He's over there."

"Ar'm sorry now ar went at 'im—an' you thaar."

"That's all right. I didn't mind."

There was a pause, while he winced and wiped away the sweat from his forehead with the back of a black hand.

"You 'is young leddy?"

"No, indeed not. Cousin. I'm staying with them, that's all."

"'Cause you aint 'is sort, ar'm thinkin'. Gord, 'e's 'ard 'e is. It's 'is kind wot makes the men gow Red."

"Oughtn't you to be quiet, don't you think?"

"Ar'll 'ave plenty o' time to be quiet in 'orspital. Ar don't orfen get t' chance o' talkin'. . . The Boss, 'e won't let yer talk. Ar'd like you to tell the Boss summat."

She indicated the men standing near.

"Ar don't mind 'em 'earin'. Ar'm dismissed now. Yer can tell the Boss it aint 'is way as'll stop the strike—'an ther mostly like 'im, the Bosses. Wot we wants is Bosses as is 'uman. It's 'uman bein's we are, not bloomin' machines. . . . If yer puts down yer pick——— Ar wor only lookin' at yer. 'Oo wudn't look at a gal like yew?"

Verna became aware of Jim's sharp voice giving orders. A couple of ambulance men came up, regarded her in a kindly way and proceeded to lift the stretcher. The big man, who had approached, superintended. Verna said quickly:

"I'll do my best, I promise. . . . And I'm going to come and see you in hospital. May I?"

She put out her hand. Morrison gripped it shakily, without speaking; and then smudged at his cheek. He noticed the big man:

"An' ar'd like t' thank yer fer comin' down t' pit an' doin' me up. Ay, 'an I'll tell yer it's not ivryone uttud———"

"That's all right," said the big man.

"An' I'd like yer name."

"Father Thornton's my name. . . . Now!"

They carried him away, the big man accompanying. Verna stood there, watching. The others followed to the ambulance which was waiting at the end of the cinder-road from the pit-head. She saw Jim coming towards her.

"Ready, Verna? . . . Hullo, what's up? . . . Lord, it's all right; these things happen every week."

Verna made no reply.

"Coming?"

"I'll walk up, if you don't mind," she answered.

A look of irritation crossed his face:

"Verna, I can't make you out today. What the devil's up?"

She flashed out suddenly:

"Oh, for the love of God, go! . . . Get away!"

Jim regarded her in amazement.

The sound of voices from the shaft-head caught his ear, and he turned. A cage-load of men had just come up from their shift. They were coming along exclaiming noisily and angrily, and did not notice him and Verna until within a few yards. Their voices suddenly dropped. They walked past without touching their caps. One of them flung back an epithet, and another something about Morrison obviously intended for Jim. He watched them, with an unpleasant gleam in his eyes.

"All right, Verna, we'll finish this later."

He followed them quickly down the cinder-road. The men were looking back over their shoulders. Jim shouted:

"Come here, you lot!"

They took no notice, but walked on. Outside the gate, on the main road, he caught them up, passing the big man who was returning. The ambulance had just driven off. Verna saw Jim plant himself in front of them. One man tried to shoulder him out of the way. The others stopped and surrounded him threateningly. She heard snarling voices and Jim beating them down stridently—"You damned Communists!" A volley of oaths came. He pushed aside a fist that was shaken in his face, hesitated, and then walked across the road to his car. There was a sudden quiet. The men were looking about them, and stooping down.

"Drop those stones!"

The big man, who had been standing with his hands in his pockets, watching, strode swiftly down the cinder-road. His shout had arrested them. They hesitated as they saw him coming, one man alone flinging a stone at the car as it moved off. The big man reached them. They surrounded him defiantly. A voice above the rest called, "'E's all right. 'E got Morrison up." There was an abrupt lull. He succeeded in pacifying them apparently; they began to walk off in twos and threes. He remained talking quietly with a couple, who touched their caps before they left.

Verna made a move, and met him at the gates. He was smiling and singularly unperturbed.

"Is it—all right?"

"Fairly," he replied.

"It was topping of you, that. My cousin's an utter——" She was going to say "cad".

"Your cousin?"

"Yes. But don't let that deter you."

Instead of expressing his opinion, he consulted his watch. She asked:

"Will you come up to the house, for tea?"

"It's very kind of you, but I've no time."

"Your face is black; you'll have to wash somewhere."

He proceeded to work with his handkerchief.

"I'm only a mile from here. Melton."

She regarded him questioningly:

"Is that where you work?"

"Well—at the moment."

"Oh?... You're a Catholic priest, Father Thornton?"

He smiled at the catechism.

"I was a surgeon first, if that will explain."

She was suddenly studying him intently; in particular, his right hand with the middle finger missing.

"Are you by any chance—— Wasn't there something about you in the paper? You're speaking in York tonight?"

"I believe so."

"Then I know who you are now. Do you mind shaking hands?"

He laughed, and did so. She told him:

"This is very strange. I was at a meeting of yours once, in London."

"Indeed?"

"I'm afraid I went—— Well, just to have a look at you. You were rather an interesting person. It was just after the Hendringham case."*

"Oh?" came drily.

* *Vide* "The Masterful Monk."

"May I tell you? I shan't keep you. Something you said, that night, stuck—about girls selling their bodies to the public. Do you remember? Otherwise I might have been a Hollywood show-girl by now. Do you understand? I was out in Hollywood."

He was looking at her in a puzzled way.

"Curiously, there was a man on the boat, coming back, who said almost the same as you; we were talking about that sort of thing."

"Captain Louis Vivien?" he asked.

She was too amazed to speak for a moment.

"But——"

He smiled:

"You are Miss Verna Wray?"

It bewildered her still more.

"His description of you was very exact."

She could only request:

"Will you enlighten one?"

"Certainly. It was Captain Vivien you met on the boat?"

"It was."

"And it was the same person who told me about you."

There was a pause.

"But, this is—— What, he's a friend of yours?"

"I met Captain Vivien at a Base hospital, in the War; and for the first time since then, in London—the other day."

She digested it.

"This is very interesting. . . . Really? And he told you about me?"

"Amongst other things about Hollywood."

She said "Oh?" slowly. "What were the 'other things'?"

Instead of answering, he glanced at his watch again:

"I must go now."

"I'm sorry, I've been keeping you. Did Captain Vivien say anything—— We met when he was in England last year."

"He told me that."

"Did he tell you what happened?"

"Yes," he answered.

Her eyes were upon his face; there was a distress appearing in the blue depths.

"Father Thornton, I'll have to meet you again. I must. . . . When?"

"Some time when I'm in London. I'll let you know. Would you give me your address?"

He produced a pencil and note-book, and wrote it down at her dictation; then remarked:

"You'll go and see Morrison? You were splendid."

"Will he die?"

"Not if they amputate properly." He stretched out his hand: "Goodbye."

Verna took it:

"It would have been horrible today, except for—— You're a monk, aren't you?"

He answered with a nod, raised his hat, and walked off towards the gates. She called: "I shall be in your audience tonight."

He smiled back.

She watched him stride away down the road.

INTERIM

The General Strike, May 1926

At a Conference of the English Labour Leaders, the final draft of the strike-notice is being read by the chairman to members listening intently round a table.

In the engine-rooms at pitheads the great wheels are still revolving to the roar of machinery.
Over industrial centres factory chimneys are still belching forth black volumes.

In a public hall in South Wales a meeting of coal-owners is in progress, unrelenting determination in each face.

At the pitheads lock-out notices are being posted up. In the engine-rooms the great wheels' revolutions have ceased.
Over industrial areas the black volumes have dwindled into wisps.
In newspaper printing-houses the presses have hummed down into silence.
Throughout England there is no sound or sight of train, or bus, or tramcar.

Outside a steel-works, on a cart, a wild-eyed being with froth at the mouth is shouting: "Comrades, they done it in Russher, and we can do it 'ere!"
In a provincial city street mounted police are making a baton charge on rioteers.
In a London thoroughfare hooligans are stoning a bus driven by a youth in plus-fours, and placarded, "Flappers, stop me."
On a railway station platform passengers are cheering an engine-driver in spats, climbing an engine and waving, "Cheerio!"

At a pub corner groups of men are standing idle, watching streams of people walking to their work.

Round London Docks, along the pavements, dockers are lounging, spitting, looking about. At a wall-angle a machine-gun is posted, with troops in place.

Past a sign-post pointing, "London—Aldershot", a battalion of Tanks is rumbling heavily through the night.

Within an Electrical Power Station naval ratings are working the plant to the tune of a popular song.

In Hyde Park a vast Milk Depot is seething with human activity.

Along a country road Food Transport lorries are pounding on their way.

In the lounge of a hotel people are listening through earphones to the Prime Minister's voice announcing the end of the strike, charged with emotion and supported by soft music in the background. A lady's eyes are raised in ecstasy. Another's hand is fumbling for a handkerchief. A man gives a sudden guffaw.

The great wheels at pitheads are revolving; factory chimneys belching; printing-presses humming; trains, buses and tramcars pursuing their way.

Chapter VIII

C APTAIN VIVIEN stopped and surveyed the scene.
There were half a dozen or so platforms, a crowd before each, and what appeared to be an immense shouting
competition in progress. He was able gradually to isolate voices
and the speakers to whom they belonged. At the Marble Arch
end, where he had entered the park, a considerable number
were around a shabby man with a narrow face, addressing them
in penetrating, nasal tones. They were mostly working-men,
with a sprinkling of young men and girls of the student type.

Captain Vivien moved nearer and listened.

"... Oi'm a workin' man, Oi am. Oi'm one of the men as was
beetrayed by 'is leaders. They calls a General Stroike, and then
they calls it orf, becorse they sees a few machine-guns abaht.
Cowards Oi call 'em. Wot we wants is leaders wot'll hact, not
tork. It's the hortumn nah, and they aint done nuffin'. Lenin,
'e hacted, 'e did. Yus, they let us dahn; but yew wait. We aint
done yet. It's a revolooshun wot's comin', same as in Russher.
They done the capiterlists dahn in Russher, and we'll do 'em
dahn 'ere." A clerical looking person passing by attracted his
attention. "Yus, and rerligion too. Rerligion, it's dope, that's
wot it is—we'll all be 'appy in 'eaven, never moind wot it's loike
dahn 'ere. Rerligion's orlrite for them wot gits paid fer it. Yus,
and 'oo pays 'em? The capiterlists! It's the capiterlists wot pays
'em, ter dope the workers. It's them with the money wot does it.
'Oo pays fer the Harmy? 'Oo pays fer the machine-guns as the

Government brings aht in the Stroike? 'Oo pays the perleece to 'it the workers abaht?"

A voice shouted, "And who pays you?" The man ignored the question and yelled louder:

"It's a revolooshun wot's comin'! Haction we wants, not tork——"

Two policemen came up, and removed him.

Captain Vivien went on.

He smiled as he caught sight of a platform exhibiting a crucifix, from which a monk, in his habit, was addressing an extensive crowd, his voice carrying strong and vibrant above others in the vicinity.

The address ended as Captain Vivien reached the place. The crowd stirred, and then became intent again. The monk was calling for questions. A man close under the platform opened with something about the Prime Minister, which Captain Vivien missed, but to which the monk replied:

"That is a purely political question, which I must refuse to answer. Next?"

Another voice called:

"Yer'e Farther Thornton, aintcher? 'Ere, does yore Church 'old with capiterlists wot grinds dahn the workers?"

The monk repeated the question to the crowd, and then answered:

"The Catholic Church condemns *any* capitalist who grinds down the workers, *any* capitalist who disregards the rights of Labour, and *any* capitalist who accumulates money-power at the expense of his workers."

"Then, wot's yore Church doin'—backin' the capiterlist?"

The monk replied:

"It depends on what you mean—'backing the capitalist'. . . Listen to this."

He produced a note-book, found a place, and read:—

"'On the one side there is the party which holds power because it holds wealth; which has in its grasp the whole of labour and trade; which manipulates for its own benefit and its own purposes all the sources of supply, and which is even represented in the Councils of the State itself.'"

He looked up to see if the questioner was attending.

"'On the other side there is the needy and powerless multitude, broken down and suffering. . . . By degrees it has come to pass that working-men have been surrendered, all isolated and helpless, to the hard-heartedness of employers and the greed of unchecked competition. . . . To this must be added . . . the concentration of so many branches of trade in the hands of a few individuals; so that a small number of very rich men have been able to lay upon the teeming masses of the labouring poor a yoke little better than that of slavery itself.'"

The monk paused, and then added:

"Does that satisfy you, sir?"

"I aint arskin' wot yew thinks, but yore Church wot backs the capiterlist."

The monk smiled:

"I've been reading to you what the Pope of Rome says. Those are the words of Pope Leo the thirteenth."

There was an abrupt silence.

"Gorblimey, 'e's a Communist."

"No. Pope Leo the thirteenth was not a Communist. That is Christian and Catholic teaching. We do not condemn capitalism as such, but the evils in the capitalistic system. We condemn the domination of money-power; the concentration of wealth in the hands of the few. We condemn unrestricted competition, profiteering, underselling, control of the Press, the sacrificing of the laws of Justice. We condemn the capitalists who gain the machinery of social life at the expense of the common good of the people—if that's what you mean by 'backing the capitalist'."

"Yer bluffin' aintcher? Yew aint a Communist?"

"I'm *not* bluffing. I'm *not* a Communist. I'm a Christian. I'm a Catholic. And I condemn Communism."

A voice from another quarter came snarlingly:

"There yer are! 'E's a capiterlist!"

The monk answered coolly:

"I am. I've some coins on me; so have you probably. We're both capitalists. My dear sir, a system is one thing, the evils in it are another. You don't shout against the human system because it suffers from diseases."

The snarler retorted:

"Yer'e side-trackin'! . . . 'E's side-trackin', 'e is!"

There was an isolated cry of, "'Ere, 'ere!"

The monk leaned forward.

"Kindly don't try that stuff on *me*. And don't try it on a crowd, every intelligent member of which can see that I'm giving straight answers. Next question?"

There was a pause, during which from the neighbouring platform could be heard: "I am appealing to English men and women. Will no man raise his voice against illegal Romanist meetings?"

Somebody shouted, "Yes, if he gets paid for it!" The reply was drowned in a burst of, "Glory, Glory, Hallelujah", from the Salvation Army on the other side. The monk was smiling broadly:

"Any more questions?"

A high-pitched female voice shrilled an enquiry as to whether he was saved, and the statement that he couldn't save others unless he was saved himself. "Shurrup!" The owner of the voice became engaged in a heated argument with those in her vicinity. "Yah, go an' drahn yerself!"

Chapter Eight

Captain Vivien took advantage of the disturbance to work his way behind a group of men to his right, whom he had been observing as he listened.

"I should be grateful if you'd hold your meeting somewhere else," the monk requested. The woman was inveigled away shrieking at all and sundry that she was saved. The snarler saw his chance:

"There yer are. That's wot rerligion does for yer! Look at 'er!"

The monk informed him:

"That's not religion. That's a noise. Any more questions?"

The original questioner returned to it:

"Yus, wot Oi wants ter know is—wot yew got ergainst Communism?"

"I've nothing against *voluntary* Communism, neither has the Catholic Church. I'm a voluntary Communist myself; I'm a monk. We share all things in common. The Catholic Church condemns *compulsory*, State Communism—a totally different thing. The State could never lawfully abolish the right of private property. That's a natural right. And a God-given right."

"Oi dunno abaht Gord. There's wot yer can git—and the workers' goin' ter git it. Wot's yore Church doin' to 'elp 'em git it?"

"Very well. Now, listen."

"Orl rite, guv'nor, Oi'll listen. But Oi could do with 'arf a pint, Oi could."

"So could I." The monk raised his voice. "The questioner asks me what the Catholic Church is doing to help the workers 'get it'—get their lawful rights. Is that it?"

"Yus, wot the capiterlists 'ave took from 'em—and wot they got back nah in Russher."

"Very good." The monk waited a moment. "The Catholic Church is steadily proclaiming those principles of Justice and

87

Charity upon which social life *must* be run if the lawful rights of Labour are to be secured. There can be no sound social system without them. And you will *not* get those principles from Russia. You will *not* get them from a system based on terrorism and force, and spelling slavery for the workers——"

"'Ere——"

"You said you would listen. . . . Whatever the Bolshevik system may do for the worker, of its very nature it can only do it at the expense of his freedom. You'll not get your freedom in that defiant, Godless way. Christian Justice and Charity are part and parcel of the Divine Code of moral law, and without them the workers will never obtain *real* freedom, or their lawful rights. That means Christianity. And Christianity means the Catholic Church."

A voice intruded itself from the Atheist platform behind:

"I ask you, my friends, why should God become Man?" A voice from the monk's crowd retorted: "Why the 'ell shouldn't 'E? Turn yer marf away!"

The monk was smiling to himself:

"If the Divine Code of moral law were running here in England, it would mean a living wage for labour, profit-sharing instead of wage-slavery, and ownership for the many instead of the few. . . . How is the Catholic Church going to help? By fighting for the *one* thing that Bolshevism and, to all appearances, Capitalists, the Press, and politicians are agreed upon to prevent—the Almighty having a say in social life. . . . And this is for all of you—If you want to shout at politicians and statesmen, shout at them to get down on their knees before Almighty God! And get down on your knees yourselves!"

A refined voice intervened:

"I thought you promised us courtesy, sir?"

"Certainly. And if it's discourteous to tell you to say your prayers, I apologise."

"'E's orl rite, 'Orace. We don't warnt no kid-gloves 'ere. Git on wiv it, guv'nor."

The monk consulted his watch:

"Thank you. I've finished. Go and get your half-pint, and God bless you."

"Gorblimey!"

The monk stepped down from the platform into the midst of some young men behind him, one of whom was waiting to take his place and who gripped his hand nervously:

"This is my first go, Father. Say a prayer for me."

"I will. God bless you. Stick your chest out."

The young man ascended, crossed himself, and began. The monk watched for a minute, smiled goodbye to the others, and made his way round the outskirts of the crowd, with heads turning as he passed. He found his way suddenly blocked by a group of men, one of whom thrust a newspaper into his face: "I believe you wrote that, sir?" His tone was insolent. The monk motioned him aside, and, with eyes ahead, forged his way through until he was clear of them. He was met by Captain Vivien. They gripped warmly.

"Go straight along, shall we?"

"The Church of God will take a taxi?"

"The Church of God will walk, if the Intelligence Service will observe."

"The men with the newspaper? Indeed, yes."

"Captain Louis, it is a great joy to see you again. Come along."

They swung off together in step, away from the noise of the platforms, veering round to the left. Feet were following. The same newspaper was again thrust before the monk's face, with:

"Would you kindly give me your attention, sir; I understand you wrote this?" The monk remarked to Captain Vivien:

"The sun lowering to the west over Hyde Park is London's greatest glory."

"We shall then keep to the Park, and walk into the glory? Padre, it is ten years since we have walked together."

"Étretat? The base hospital. We walked into the sunset, then." Audible rude remarks were being flung after them by the men behind.

"Through the trees," Captain Vivien contributed. "With the flies buzzing round. Two of them already have gone back."

"How do you know?"

"Because now there are only three pairs of feet walking." A final sneering epithet came, and the sound of feet ceased. They walked on together in silence, until the monk asked:

"Anything more?"

"I will tell you," said Captain Vivien. "The man with the newspaper has a boil on his neck."

The monk laughed, and turned enquiringly.

"Because, while you are speaking, I stand behind his neck in the crowd. It is after the lady with the noise who is saved, when he says to the others that you are the damned monk from Italy. He is angry because you finish suddenly, before he can get back to the Atheist platform from which he comes. I think he has intended to say to his crowd, while you stand there— this is the man who has insulted England in this newspaper. . . . But I do not know what you have written."

The monk informed him:

"Only that England's morals are little better than Russia's."

"That is bold."

"And that respectable immorality is less honest."

"That is bolder."

"Captain Louis, you've to hit an Englishman mighty hard— to make him as honest with himself as he is with others."

Captain Vivien considered.

"In France we say that Englishmen see what it is convenient to see." He laughed to himself. "I say to a business-man yesterday—you are an English Bolshevik, and he thinks that I am not polite. So I ask him—but you say to me there is no moral law, the marriage-bond, bah! Is not that Bolshevism? You are a rebel against Christian civilisation. He is angry then: 'Christian civilisation be damned!' And I answer—that is what the Bolsheviks say. Goodbye."

He halted and looked back. The monk did the same. On the right of the Marble Arch the crowds were still listening round the platforms. Above the heads a figure was discernible brandishing something white, and emphasizing with it.

Captain Vivien remarked:

"So now he tells the British public about the insolent monk."

They walked on again.

The monk asked:

"Lancaster Gate?"

"It is further past Lancaster Gate, the flat," Captain Vivien told him.

"What exactly is the programme?"

"After I take you inside, I shall go. Miss Harwood will be out, so Verna will talk with you more freely."

There was an interval.

"Louis."

"Yes?"

"You're just as fond of her?"

Louis affirmed:

"I do not change in this—in my love for Verna. I shall not change, whatever it is that happens."

"But you consider yourselves free, both of you?"

"That is the agreement."

"And your stipulation stands?"

"Indeed, yes. I am most firm."

"Thank you."

Captain Vivien slipped his arm through the monk's:

"You will not object that the Intelligence Service advises that we walk now outside, by the Bayswater Road?"

"What's the idea?"

"Because it is better that the man who is following you does not know where you go, or they will say the damned monk from Italy goes to a lady's flat. You are being shadowed, *mon ami.*"

"Shadowed? . . . This is very interesting."

"Please you will not look round. You shall see in one minute a man who has a bad name with the Intelligence Service, and who is now walking a little way behind on the other side of the railings . . . If you please, Padre, to the right . . . We will stop at the gate, so that I light a cigarette. You understand?"

They veered to the right. The monk saw a man in a grey suit who was coming along the pavement, slow down. At the gate, Captain Vivien took out his cigarette case and stood there to light up, his eyes resting carelessly on the grey-suited figure, who now had no choice but to turn back or pass on ahead. He did the latter, quickening his pace. The monk had a glimpse of a sallow-skinned face with high cheekbones. They waited until he was well on in front. Captain Vivien remarked:

"It is always amusing to follow the man who is following you."

They emerged through the gate and continued to the left along the pavement, with the man fifty yards ahead.

"That was clumsy," the monk observed.

"And why do you say so?"

"An ordinary passer-by would have looked."

"At a monk in his habit? Padre, you will join the Intelligence Service?"

The monk asked:

"Who is he? A Russian?"

"So you observe the face of Mr. Cavenor whose name is Karenov when he is in Moscow."

"Indeed? That man was in the crowd just now. You know?"

"But not with the newspaper men; and yet he leaves the crowd to speak to the man with the boil, when you come down. . . . My Padre, it is for more than the newspaper that a Bolshevik agent employs men to quarrel with you. You will be careful; because it is not the first time that I follow him when he follows you."

"Oh?" said the monk.

Captain Vivien's eyes had not left the man in front:

"He is very anxious to look round. . . . He is thinking very hard."

"The uneven stride?"

"Padre, you will most certainly join the Intelligence Service. . . . He is thinking very hard . . . but he must not look round . . . before he crosses the road, which I think he will do. . . . This bus, it is stopping here? . . . Yes . . . We will climb to the top . . . quickly."

They boarded the bus.

Captain Vivien followed up the stairs with:

"And so we are vanished."

On the top he said:

"And next we get down at the flat."

CHAPTER IX

THE MONK put his cup down.

His eyes strayed again round the room. Miss Verna Wray had indubitably good taste in pictures. In everything, if "my drawing-room"—she had called it—were an index.

Artistically, it was flawless. He had observed the titles of some of the books; suggestive of ethical aspirations. She was different from his first impression of her on that day at the pithead in Yorkshire. There was an indefinable quality of character underlying the film-star appearance of the girl Captain Louis loved.

He noticed a photograph on the mantelpiece.

"That's Terry," she informed him.

"The 'staid companion'?"

She laughed.

"Did Louis tell you that? Yes; my guardian angel."

The monk leaned back in his chair. Their eyes met.

"Now, start."

Verna stood up and moved the tea-table out of the way. She lit a cigarette, and then rested an elbow on the mantelpiece.

"Father Thornton, you won't mind if I talk about myself?"

"Carry on."

"Well—you said, that afternoon, Louis had told you."

"Yes. By the way, what happened to Morrison?"

"I saw Morrison in hospital, and I've heard from him since. He's a cripple, living on his insurance now."

"How is he taking it?"

"He's done what you told him."

"Come back to his religion?"

"Yes. I was to tell you—he's a 'good Catholic' again."

"That's splendid! . . . Yes?"

Verna hesitated.

"Father Thornton, what did Louis say? I've not asked him."

The monk told her:

"Quite briefly, that he was very much in love with you, and that he had asked you to marry him, assuming you would become a Catholic. That is, if you consented."

"Did he tell you I only realised that, after I had said yes?"

"I gathered it came to you as a shock."

"Very much so. I didn't even know it was in his mind. I supposed it was his French outlook . . . Anyway, I refused to become a Catholic in order to marry him."

"And he was adamant on your being one—first?"

"Yes."

He knew, more or less, but he asked her:

"What's the position at the moment?"

"Things are at a deadlock. He's been here of course, since he was back. We've been to a show together; we're perfectly friendly. We simply don't refer to it, because there's nothing to discuss. . . . But it's all so utterly stupid."

"Hardly stupid," he disagreed.

"Well, futile."

"To go on seeing him?"

"Yes, if we can never marry. It hurts—horribly, both of us. We're desperately in love the whole time." Her tone was curiously matter of fact.

The monk helped himself to a cigarette from a silver box on the table, and lit it slowly. His grey eyes fixed hers.

"Now, tell me what it really is?"

She stood upright from her leaning posture.

"What do you mean?"

"What I say. Tell me what it really is?"

For a moment she looked like taking offence.

"You give no hint of considering what he asks."

"But I don't intend to consider it."

"Why not?"

"Become a Catholic to marry him!"

"Not in *order* to marry him. You could become a Catholic *and* marry him."

"I couldn't——I can't!"

"Exactly. Tell me what it is."

Her lips were suddenly quivering. She threw her cigarette end into the fire.

"Father Thornton, I wanted you to help me."

"I can't help you, unless you help me."

"Why shouldn't Louis give in? It's only a matter of getting a dispensation."

He shook his head.

"For a mixed marriage? He wouldn't consent."

"If you told him, he would."

She was pleading now.

"I shall not tell him," the monk said firmly. "You're asking me to override his perfectly sincere conviction—with which I agree, as a matter of fact."

"You'd approve of a dispensation in another case."

He shrugged his shoulders:

"Not in yours."

There was a dead silence.

Verna walked slowly away, and made a pretence of straightening the cover of a chair. She sat down hesitatingly. The monk remarked:

"You see, I don't think it's prejudice. You live with a Catholic."

He nodded at a Madonna on the wall draped with a string of Rosary beads.

"Oh no, I've nothing against the Catholic religion."

"But you won't look at it?"

"Why should I?" came with a note of defiance.

The monk plunged:

"You would under the circumstances, if——"

He asked outright, "What's keeping you back?"

She leaned forward with her hand over her eyes. Her lips were trembling again.

"Would you rather I went?"

"N—no. But you're—— Why are you insisting like this?"

"Because you want me to help you."

For a moment she was perilously near tears. He looked away. She succeeded in controlling herself, and looked up. Her manner suddenly became resolute.

"Very well. . . . Father Thornton, something happened—just before Louis asked me."

"Last year?"

"Yes. Did he tell you about my people?"

The monk nodded:

"There'd been trouble, yes."

"Over a man I refused to marry—a Harland Carville. I came here to live with Terry because of it." She went on quickly: "I ran into my people in Oxford Street, in November. We hadn't seen each other since I left home, and—I don't know, I suppose they saw the silliness of it all, meeting me suddenly like that . . . Anyway, we had tea together, and they suggested my coming back home again; so I had to tell them about Louis. I'd had a letter from him making it plain enough what he would ask me, when he reached England. They seemed quite pleased; at any rate they didn't mind his being French. We parted almost affectionately at Charing Cross. But the pater asked at the last moment whether Louis was a Catholic. I told him—naturally; he was French."

"Yes?" the monk encouraged.

"I didn't see the significance, until a letter came. They wanted to know whether I had any intention of becoming a Catholic myself."

"What was your answer?"

She hesitated.

"That it was quite possible I might, as I'd already been considering the question." She went on rather breathlessly, "Father Thornton, don't think of me too hardly; because you'll understand now—but the pater wrote straight back that if I became a Catholic, he would allow me nothing, and nothing whatever would come to me. They're v—very well off." Her head lowered.

The monk's grey eyes were on the wall in front. He remarked after a while:

"It's been brave of you to tell me."

"That's not all," she said.

"No?"

"I met somebody—somebody you know; after Louis had left England again. At Christmas. I was spending it with some friends in Herefordshire, and they took me to a place called Morton. We had tea with your friends—the Campions."

"You met June Campion."

Verna looked up.

"She told you?"

"I was there two weeks ago."

"Were you really? . . . Did she—Father Thornton, she's rather an intuitive person, isn't she?"

"The blind do become intuitive. Yes?"

"She knew somehow that I wanted to get her away to talk alone. We went into another room. I asked her about herself first, and she told me about the accident and her blindness, and then all about Cyril Rodney and you—in Russia. At least—— Father, what exactly happened?"

He told her:

"Major Rodney was crucified in a forest beyond Archangel, by some Reds."

"Crucified?"

"He refused the alternative they gave him—of insulting a crucifix."

She remained silent.

"I see . . . And you?"

"Does it matter? I was left to die of exposure; a search-party found me in time."

"Oh? . . . Then you actually saw it?"

"They'd bound me to a tree opposite."

There was another silence.

"Major Rodney had become a Catholic just before, hadn't he?"

"Yes."

"I suppose his Faith cost him his life?"

"Yes."

"I gathered that. It was why I couldn't tell her about myself and my people; although I'd intended to. I felt she would despise me."

"June Campion's not that kind," he affirmed.

"Don't *you* despise me? After Major Rodney?"

"It's not my business to 'despise' you." He said it almost impatiently. She stared at him.

"Do you quite understand? I *should* be a Catholic, only I'd lose everything. I've only mentioned June Campion because she made me feel completely contemptible, and I want you to realise that I *am*; in my own eyes. I'm not blind to myself. I'd no intention of letting you know all this; but you've practically made me. And I'd sooner you'd find no excuses. I can't do it—that's all. I told Louis once that I'm worldly; and I *am*—utterly, hopelessly worldly."

As he made no comment, she added:

"I suppose Louis should know? What I've told you?"

"It would be fair to let him know, yes."

He looked at his watch, and rose.

"I'll have to get back."

The abruptness of it surprised her. She took the hand he held out, mechanically. He said, "Goodbye," and walked towards the door.

"But——"

The monk turned enquiringly.

"But, aren't you—— I thought——"

He waited. She said rather feebly:

"I thought you'd have more to say."

"Is there anything more to say? You've put the position very clearly."

A flash of anger showed itself:

"Then you've made me tell all this—for nothing."

"Oh, no," came quietly.

"Then, why?"

"You wanted me to help you?"

"I did."

"When you let me, I will."

He had gone, closing the door behind him.

.　　　.　　　.　　　.　　　.

"I've told Father Thornton everything."

Terry switched on the light, and began removing her gloves.

"Tophole! Everything what?"

"Oh, about Louis and myself."

Verna continued to fiddle restlessly with an ornament on the mantelpiece. Terry perched herself on the arm of the sofa.

"He made me. He's—disgustingly overbearing."

"No doubt. But, everything what about Louis and yourself?"

Verna wheeled round:

"Terry, I'm——"

She stopped short.

"No, I can't—— I can't tell you . . . I will—some time. It's——
Oh, why the devil should one be expected——" She flung out
of the room, closing the door with a slam.

Chapter X

A VISTA OF the Penn Ponds glittering in the autumn sun, opened before them. They stood there for a moment, watching. There were some deer making across the slope half way down. On the road below, to the right, their car was parked; they could see the chauffeur lighting a cigarette. Captain Vivien did the same himself.

They moved on. The gates of the White Lodge appeared on their left. They passed them, crossing the road, and then made on up the hill through the bracken—both of them uncomfortably silent.

At the top Captain Vivien surveyed. There were some isolated trees ahead, and, beyond them, a downward incline of russet and yellow woodland enclosed in fencing. He pointed in the direction with his stick. They walked on in the same selfconscious silence.

At the trees he halted and looked about. There was a trunk which had been felled and left to lie.

"We will sit on the fallen tree?"

"It will be appropriate," Verna replied.

He glanced at her as he led the way:

"And how?"

"For a fallen woman." She waited until they had established themselves on the trunk. "Very shortly, I shall be a fallen woman in your eyes. . . . Louis, do you remember saying to me once that I had great ideals? I told you I was hopelessly worldly?"

"On the boat from New York, yes."

He was watching her profile.

"I'm going to fall right down with a crash from my pedestal; but you put me on it, remember."

Louis said quietly:

"And I shall keep you on the pedestal. So you have told the Padre?"

She swung round, facing him:

"How do you know?"

"Oh, no, he has said nothing. It is only that Padre Thornton would insist; that is his way."

He inhaled deeply from his cigarette, and then flung it away.

"My Verna, I have understood always that it was more than the religion itself; but I have not understood why you keep it from me."

She answered without looking at him:

"Because a woman likes to be idealised, by the man she loves. You'll not idealise me, and you'll find the real woman anything but lovable——"

"I shall love you always. The Great Romance, it is for always between you and me."

Verna remained still for a moment, then moved nearer and laid her hands on his shoulders. She drew his head down and kissed him:

"Louis, oh my Louis, you're going to get a terrible shock." She drew a deep breath. "Yes, I told Father Thornton. I didn't mean to, but he more or less made me. He wouldn't consider what I wanted—you to give in."

"I am glad."

"Louis, I *should* be a Catholic, and he knew it at once. I should be a Catholic now—if I were free."

He evinced no surprise.

"If you were free?"

She said in rather a forced voice:

"Yes. There's a very big thing in the way, Louis."

He asked in the same quiet way:

"Bigger than the Faith?"

Her hands left his shoulders. She looked towards the woodland below.

"You're making it more difficult for me."

"That is good."

She appeared not to understand:

"How do you mean?"

"Because I do not want it to be easy for you to tell me that you prefer something to *le bon Dieu*."

"Louis! Don't!"

"But it is that?"

She hesitated.

"Need you put it so—crudely? It hurts."

"That also is good—that it hurts."

She turned with a sudden flash of anger:

"I don't know what——I've told Father Thornton that I'm utterly contemptible in my own eyes. Isn't that enough?"

"Oh, no, it is not enough," came coolly.

She stared at him.

"I don't understand——I'm going to tell you; and it will be the most humiliating——"

"But I do not think that I wish to know."

She sat upright, facing him.

"Louis, what's up? You're rude!"

He shrugged his shoulders, and watched a leaf zig-zagging downwards. She asked sharply:

"What do you think I've brought you out here for?"

He smiled:

"I think you have brought me out here, to Richmond Park, because it will be more romantic like this." He waved his stick at the scene around. "Louis and Verna will sit amongst the trees and the falling leaves of autumn, and the birds will sing. It will all be very sad. And Verna will tell Louis that she is the most despicable of women, because the sacrifice of something is too big for her; and she will put her arms round his neck and implore him that he will not think too badly of her, but they must part for ever, because now she will be contemptible in his eyes. And Louis will gaze at her, and his heart will be torn between love and his duty. She will——"

"Louis!——"

"She will sob upon his breast, and Louis' heart will begin to soften. He will say—'It is too much. I cannot let my Verna go. I must find a way—somehow.'"

"Louis! . . . Louis, how *dare* you!"

"But Louis will not say that. There will be no—somehow."

She sprang up, and flung away from him; then turned to vent her anger.

"No, please you will control yourself."

The sternness in his manner checked her. The fury did not come. There was a moment of indecision; and then she burst into tears . . .

Louis remained sitting there, swinging his stick. He waited until she had found her handkerchief.

"Come back, because I have not finished."

"You're c—cruel. You're utterly cruel!"

"I do not think so. Because if you will not understand me, then most certainly it will be goodbye."

"Y—you've never sneered at me before."

"I have not sneered at you now, because I show you what you do not wish to see."

She continued crying quietly, and the stick continued swinging. He studied the view, until, at length, she came back, slowly, and sat down, away from him. He watched her repairing the havoc of the tears.

"You don't even know. I've told you nothing."

"It is a habit of the Intelligence Service to know, when we have been told 'nothing'. But I do not wish you to tell me anything more."

She was looking at him in a startled way:

"Has my father——"

"Oh no, he has not. It is because you emphasize that you are worldly, and because you say that it is very big, I arrive at the conclusion that there are some very big worldly prospects in the way. I do not, however, wish to know more."

He silenced her attempt to speak with a gesture:

"I have said the Great Romance it is for always between you and me; and it shall be if you wish it. But it is with you now—and *le bon Dieu*."

Her head lowered.

"Tomorrow I go from England; but I shall take with me in my heart the ideal of my Verna, who will be always upon the pedestal."

The heel of her shoe began screwing about. She looked up at him:

"You can say that, Louis? After——"

"But I can. Louis says to himself, perhaps he would be the same; it is the revolt of human nature when *le bon Dieu* asks for the very big thing . . . Come here, my Verna."

She moved nearer.

"Close . . . because I love you."

She was by his side. He took her face between his hands and raised it; then kissed her reverently on the lips.

"The Padre says to me—your Verna has a heart of gold, but you will be patient."

Her surprise was unfeigned:

"He said—*that?*"

Louis nodded:

"The Padre understands, more perhaps——"

"I thought——"

"More perhaps than my Verna thinks."

She remained with her eyes on his, saying nothing, the dawn of some great wonderment in the violet depths. Her head laid itself on his shoulder. After a while a sigh came. She sat up restlessly and looked away to the woodland below, where the sun's rays were burnishing the autumn golds. There was a long silence before she moved and put her arms round his neck.

"Louis, I'm sorry . . . I'm terribly sorry . . . I'm—I'm going to try."

He kissed her, with a smile.

"So that the Great Romance, it comes true?"

There was a wisp over her ear. He played with it:

"My little schoolgirl, of the straw hair."

INTERIM

In a room within the Kremlin in Moscow, a man is seated at a desk. From the wall opposite Lenin, his predecessor, looks down. The man's forehead, beneath short dark hair, is furrowed, and his lips are sternly pursed. Before him a map of Russia is spread open. His hand is resting on a paper which contains a list of names.

In the street below, a couple of workers, leaning against a wall, are watching a funeral approaching. The scarlet hearse moves slowly by.

"Why have they shot him?"

The other jerks his head at the Kremlin above:

"Ask Stalin."

Within the hall of a Bureau at Odessa, whose walls are papered with brilliant coloured posters, a group of men and women are examining new designs.

An artist in overalls, with a cigarette between his lips, is pinning one up on an empty space. He steps back to indicate its points with a drawing carbon. There are murmurs of approval. It is headed, "The Triumph of Christianity", and represents a huge golden cross being borne by workers with bent backs and chained feet, lured on by Christ in front. On the upper side of the cross is straddled a repulsively corpulent capitalist.

The artist proceeds to pin up a second, depicting Christ advancing enticingly upon a worker. Behind Him are soldiery with fixed bayonets. It is headed, "The Secret of Christ". The poster is greeted with appreciative guttural laughter.

A third is unrolled and displayed: A horde of humanity is struggling and thrusting blindly up the back of a cliff towards Christ at the top holding aloft a blazing chalice, clutching vainly as they reach Him, before losing their foothold to be hurled, a human cascade, down into the depths below. It is inscribed, "The Saviour of the World".

One of the group spits his congratulations, and proceeds to pick his nose.

Outside the Cathedral, at Borisoglybsk, men and women, ankle-deep in snow, are crying and pleading with a Communist official. An old peasant woman, clutching a shawl round her shoulders wails: "We have no bread, nothing to eat or drink." A man calls: "We have no work, no money, only our church. And now they take that!" The official shrugs indifferently: "You have hidden the property of your church. It is the Soviet order to close the church." Another, with a wild glitter in his eyes, yells: "The Soviet is the enemy of our religion! They take it from us. Our children will have no God."

He makes a rush and hurls himself at the official, who thrusts him away, and shouts. A dozen armed soldiers are on the spot immediately. The man is clubbed to the ground with the butt-end of a gun.

In the market-square of a village, around a co-operative store, peasants, in shaggy fur caps and high boots, are surging. A man is pushing his way in: "Bread! We want bread!" Another is struggling to emerge: "Bread? The devil take you! Where is it?" A woman shrills from amongst the carts in the background: "The Jew has bread! Black bread. He wants twenty-three kopecks a foont!" She directs attention to a stand on which a large slab of it is exhibited, amidst cakes of coloured soap. "And his foont is not even a foont."

There are more cries:

"They have bread in the cities."

"The Communists have bread."
"The Peasants have no bread."

Up the stairs of a Textile tenement in Moscow, a man and woman are climbing wearily. They reach the first-floor, knock on a door, open it, and look round. Five beds are stretched round the walls. The occupants of the room stare challengingly:
"There are five husbands and five wives here."
The man and woman retire, proceed along the corridor, and open another door. A hubbub of voices dies down.
"The corner is not occupied?"
"The corner is for the Devil. Go away."
They do so. On the next stairs up, a man passes them, descending:
"It is useless. There are a hundred people on the second floor."
They reach it and look into the first room. A family is drinking tea. Two others are disputing a space. A man on a stool is examining an electric bulb.
"Go to the new buildings!"
"Yes, go to the Ideal Workers' Homes!"
"We are not Communists."
"Then you will not find a room in Moscow."
The man on the stool surveys them compassionately.
"Stay here."

Behind a counter, at the Saks Bureau of Kiev, two clerks are sitting. Before them a line of couples are awaiting their turn. One of the clerks is questioning a pair:
"When was the marriage?"
"We have been married for six weeks. I have no longer any taste for him."

The clerk opens and consults a ledger.
"I am agreed that my wife and I separate."
The clerk nods mechanically, and begins to write.
"It will cost . . ."
The second clerk motions to the next pair.

At Feofany monastery within the heart of the forest, an official is showing a foreign visitor round the outside. Byzantine domes and cupolas glitter above the sombre darkness of the trees.

"The Black monks are gone?"

"The Black monks are working. It is better than praying."

They pass through a portico, and inside.

"The monasteries are for education. So we use them."

The official leads the way through the empty hall down a corridor.

"I will show you the club-room."

He flings open a door. There is a sudden cessation of voices. The visitor finds himself in a spacious place, obviously the Refectory of former days, with the monks' tables still in position. Boys and girls look up at them from games and occupations. Some are neatly dressed, others unkempt and wild-looking. The official gestures proudly: "You will see how the system improves the deserted children." He singles out a ragged pair, dirty and unwashed: "They have come here yesterday only"; then beckons a smart youth forward: "And you have been for how long, at Feofany? . . . Five years? . . . It is——"

"What the devil——!"

The official turns at the visitor's exclamation.

"Yes, it is necessary, that they may be good Communists." The visitor is staring at the walls around, lined with posters depicting various horrors—Englishmen torturing negroes, chopping off heads, and drinking whisky; Americans and British executing

Chinese, French burning Riffs at the stake, White Russians massacring Reds. Black-jacks, knuckle-dusters and knives enhance the scheme of decoration.

"It is for the education of these children, whom the Soviet State has reclaimed."

Across the ice of the frozen Volga a man in furs is walking with a peasant whose beard mingles grey with his sheepskins. The cliffs at Yaroslavl rise before them, crowned to the skyline with broken churches.

"I have not walked by way of the ice since the Revolution."

The old man nods understandingly:

"The angels weep for Yaroslavl."

"Perhaps from above they do not see the desolation?"

They become absorbed in the sight ahead—battered domes, topless towers, twisted golden crosses, the remains of riotously coloured cupolas catching the light. The old man breaks the silence:

"The guns of the Reds have destroyed the roofs; in the War I have seen them falling. The Church of Saints Peter and Paul is everywhere guano from the birds; I have looked inside. I have also seen the Church of the Transfiguration and the posters of the Soviet on the walls; it is, inside, a workmen's shop. The snow falls upon the vestments of the priests where they have been thrown in the Church of the Nativity. From above they see everything. I am glad that I am not an angel."

Inside a modernised Soviet factory, the Communist manager stands surveying the recently installed machinery, listening to the steady throb of its revolutions, the purr of steel wheels. He turns his gaze upon the lines of workers in their places, noting their sure, efficient movements; then strolls slowly down the great interior *with his hands behind his back, nodding to himself approvingly. At the further end he consults his watch, passes through a doorway, and up a short flight of stairs to a private room, where a meal is in readiness and a contractor awaiting him. They greet each other.*

"I have watched you through the window inspecting the machinery. You are pleased?"

"The machinery is perfect. We will drink to it. Comrade, my contractor, I have had a vision just now. I have seen the factory symbolical of Russia. We have removed the old machinery, as the Revolution has removed the old regime. We have installed the new machinery, as we have installed the Bolshevik State; and the machinery now runs smoothly, as also does—— What is that?"

A sharp rattle of musketry has caught his ear. The contractor strolls to the window.

"It is the execution of some Kulaki—that is all."

The manager listens as a second volley comes, and then remarks:

"It is the machinery of the State running perfectly, as it runs here perfectly, where there is no individualism. Come and see."

They cross to the window which looks upon the interior of the factory. The manager points:

"Look! They are all part of the machinery—the Communist workers. It is perfect."

He turns to the contractor:

"There will be no individualists, no Kulaki in Russia, soon. There will be collective farming, just as the industry is collective. Russia will be the greatest nation in the world . . . There is much noise outside."

They go to the other window, and look down on the street below. A mob of frenzied men and women are shaking fists and gesticulating wildly at a platoon of the Red Army marching by.

"Come, we will drink to the machinery which runs so smoothly."

CHAPTER XI

I
N THE MAIN ROOM of a building off the Red Square in Moscow, the members of a Committee were seated at a table. It was a long table with a scarlet cloth. There were typed papers lying before each. On the wall behind the president, who was speaking, were lithographs of Karl Marx, Lenin and Stalin. There were smaller ones of Rykov and Tomsky.

The President paused, and picked up a manuscript:

"From England."

He began to read:

"'. . . Since my last report to the Committee, two hundred more young children are having instruction, and many between fourteen and eighteen in years are within "The Young Communists League". Our journals have a greater circulation, and the organizations are increasing.'"

The man next the president on his left asked:

"From whom is the report?"

The president looked up:

"From Karenov."

"Karenov reports progress always, so that he may receive more roubles," the man stated. "The English newspapers do not confirm what he says."

There were murmurs of disapproval. A man opposite disagreed:

"The English newspapers are capitalist, so they do not

advertise Communism. Karenov is a good worker."

The president rapped on the table, and continued to read:

"'I have also to report that I have the dossier complete now of the man about whom I have written. He is a monk from the Italian monastery of Issano; but he is English, and I find that he has done the work of speaking in England before, against Julian Verrers the rationalist, who died. In London this monk lives at the House of a Religious Order, but he works as well in many parts of England, in public halls and theatres and also out-of-doors. He has always large crowds to listen to him, because he is a powerful speaker, and because the newspapers have printed a story about him when he was at Archangel with the British Force which was with the Whites against us in the Civil War. In the British Force he was a Medical Officer, it is said. It is said also in the account which I have read, that some Comrades decoy him with a friend, an English Major Rodney, also that they employ a woman for this purpose to entice them to her rescue from the Comrades' hands, which happens. Afterwards these two are taken into the forest, where the Medical Officer is fixed to a tree by the Comrades while his friend is crucified. It was intended that the Medical Officer die of exposure, but he was found and brought back by an English party. I do not know if the story is true, but if it is so then it is a bad thing for us that the Comrades did not do their work better; because it is a story which has placed this monk, who was the Medical Officer, in favour here, especially because it is told by the newspapers that he has risked his life to save a woman from the Reds. The English Comrades are fools in their sentiments, because they listen now to him when he goes to Tyneside in the North of England and in other places, if they have read this story. Comrade M—— informs me so. There is also——'"

"Karenov is long-winded. Have we to listen to all this?" the man on the left interrupted. The savage note in his voice caused heads to turn. The president rapped again and went on:

"'There is also another story of this monk, that he goes down into a coal-mine to bring up an injured man, which has also placed him in favour. I have traced the publication of these stories to a man of the monk's religion, who is employed with an Association of the Press in London, and who also endeavours that his speeches are reported in the newspapers, as it has happened many times. The speeches of the monk are against Communism, and against the Bolshevik State, for which purpose he has an intimate knowledge of our system and our Code of Law; but he also teaches a programme of social reform, which is that of the Catholic Church. He is persuasive and steady in his manner, which the English also like, and not wild like the Comrades, which they say is vulgar. It is for these reasons that he is able to have a strong influence and to draw away the Comrades who listen, and who are fools.'"

The interrupter broke in sharply: "Karenov also is a fool. Why does he not remove this monk? For what do we pay him?" The president ignored him:

"'I have many times followed this monk after he has been speaking in London, because it is necessary to find out something which can be printed in our journals here against him and which the Comrades can say from their platforms; but it is difficult because he knows now that I follow him. He turns one day, and comes back to confront me, and he says that he hopes I shall not become tired, because he will walk three miles. He is clever. I do not understand how he has known.'"

"I have said Karenov was a fool. Why do you not——"

"You will be silent, if you please," the president snapped out. "We are in Committee."

He continued:

"'But it is very necessary that the monk shall be prevented from his influence against us. I have employed some men to make the crowd angry against him in Hyde Park in London about what he has written in a newspaper; but it is not enough, for the crowd remain like cows. These English, I am tired of them, with their bourgeois sentiments. They listen to the monk because he speaks of their homes and their families and their marriages which will be destroyed by the Communistic State. You of the Moscow Committee do not understand the English, when you send me here to effect revolt for Bolshevism. They are cows and sheep, the English, with whom we cannot effect revolt. We shall not in this way make a Bolshevik State in England, because the sentiments and the ideals are opposed to the materialistic philosophy which is ours, and which is necessary that Bolshevism may grow, as Lenin has taught.

"'I write so, because there is need for another direction to us than to effect revolt, which will not be accomplished. I have watched the Comrades foaming from the mouth at only twelve to listen. They waste their time. You will, I ask you, express to the Committee that the direction shall be given to Comrade M—— that he will employ men who will speak better, and who will be more educated and not wild. The English people will not accept the materialistic philosophy which must be first, except the moral ideas change. They go to the churches only a little, but the amusement-life is very popular; so I advise that our endeavour shall be with the Theatres and Cinemas and Variety Houses.

"'It is of importance that the restrictions shall be removed, and that the people shall be given everything, you understand. Already it is free-love which they see, and the ideas which are against Christian marriage, and they begin to understand that without clothes it is art and science, and so the ideas change now.

"'For this I express to the Committee that they shall employ for England the men who are "gentlemen" (it is the English word) and who will make a good appearance. Already I have approached some men who have influence, and who have the ideas of Bolshevism that England shall be Godless without Christian morality; but the money will be necessary if they work for the amusement-life to be made for that purpose.

"'The caricature-posters of Christ and the Trinity which the Committee have sent, I have employed once; but there has been an outcry in some newspapers, and the police have discovered nearly, before I have destroyed them. So I ask that the Committee shall not send more. England is not for the posters; but in the amusement-life they will be influenced, because it will not be violent like the posters, and the ideas grow better so. The English writer, H. G. Wells, has the idea well that Christian morality shall go.

"'I have no more which it is of importance to report, but I ask again that the Committee will be agreed to give the money that the work upon the amusement-life shall be done, and that I arrange with the men whom I have approached.

"'About the monk I ask that I shall be given direction, because I have not the commission to act, as it is done in Russia; you understand me. I do not know for how long he is in England, but it is for many months, because it is in a Catholic newspaper that he goes to Lourdes in France with a pilgrimage of the English next year in the Spring.

"'My greetings are to the Committee.'"

The president laid down the report, took off his spectacles, wiped and replaced them. He looked down the table:

"The Committee will express themselves about the money . . . It is agreed?"

The man who had been interrupting found his tongue:

"It is always money for Karenov! Have I not said that the Committee should send to England another agent who will do more work and spend less money?"

The president replied drily:

"And it is Roslavl who will do more work and spend less money?"

The man retorted:

"I will act as it is done in Russia, with this monk, and I will not ask for a rouble."

Two or three raised their heads. The rest fingered their papers. The man suddenly stood up, and almost shouted:

"Because the story is true! There were six Comrades who were in the forest of Archangel, and Roslavl was one!"

There was an abrupt cessation of rustling. They were staring at him now intently. The president watched him for a moment, and then asked:

"That is so?... Truly, Roslavl?"

Roslavl's fist struck the table:

"Were not the English guns at Seletskoe beyond the forest of Archangel, from where the escape was made? I have told you so before."

The president leaned back and studied him.

"It is for a good reason then that you wish to go to England?"

"It is a good reason because it was a blunder that he did not die—the Medical Officer who is now this monk."

The president considered.

"You are asking for the Commission from the Committee? So that the blunder . . . Yes, I understand." He looked about: "But, first, it is agreed that the money shall be given to Karenov to employ?"

They signified their assent, Roslavl included.

The secretary, at the president's right, made a note.

"You will be careful for what commission you ask," the president warned. Roslavl replied:

"I ask that the Committee send me to England, that is all."

"'To work according to the occasion'? It is the formal phrase."

"To work according to the occasion," Roslavl repeated.

There was a pause. The president addressed the Committee:

"You will signify—as you wish. Shall the Commission be given to Roslavl?"

They signified in the affirmative, with one exception. The dissentient averred:

"It is dangerous, this—in England."

Roslavl answered him:

"I am not a fool to endanger the Committee."

The president asked him:

"You will be one of Karenov's 'gentlemen'?" It was greeted with laughter. He said sternly:

"The beard will be shaved. And you will learn English more?"

Roslavl spread a pair of thick-fingered hands:

"Have I not understood everything which you have read from Karenov? But I will learn English more, on the way."

The president nodded reassuringly at the dissentient:

"You will signify?"

After a moment's hesitation he did so.

The secretary made another note, and the president stood up:

"The Committee is closed."

They rose, gathering up their papers, and filed out of the room in pairs or singly. The president remained standing there, with Roslavl still seated, a pen between his teeth in a nonchalant manner. The other said slowly:

"It is lawful by the Code, when Bolshevism is hindered in Russia, because it is then the death penalty. But you will be very careful, and you will be wise to remember the English law."

Roslavl nodded.

The beady eyes had become black slits.

CHAPTER XII

TERRY LOOKED about the vestibule. There was a gold-braided individual in the corner. She went up to him:

"Where's the manager?"

The man drew himself up.

"The manager, Miss?"

"I said, the manager. The manager of this cinema."

The gold-braided person crossed the vestibule to consult a boy in buttons, who disappeared. There was an uncomfortable wait, during which the girl behind the glass of the box-office became interested to the extent of a lift of the eyebrows. An embarrassed Verna, in the background, studied the picture of a film-star's head and shoulders appearing out of a bath. A business-like man in an immaculate morning coat arrived with the boy in buttons. The gold-braided person indicated Terry, who turned quickly. The manager asked suavely:

"You wished to see me?"

"Yes. I want my money back. Three and six. The're two of us. Seven shillings."

"I beg your pardon?"

"We paid seven shillings to be entertained—not insulted."

The manager maintained his *savoir-faire*.

"Certainly . . . Quite so . . . Yes, quite so."

He smoothed his knuckles ingratiatingly, inviting further explanation.

"You see your own dirty pictures, don't you?" Terry snapped.

The manager for a second was nonplussed. He endeavoured to look pleasant. The person in gold-braid put his hand to his mouth and coughed.

"Perhaps you object to something——"

"*Object?*. . . object to a filthy——"

She walked across to the box-office:

"Seven shillings, please."

The girl inside regarded her with sophisticated composure.

The manager recovered his dignity and advanced:

"Give the lady seven shillings."

The girl found the money and did so. Terry put it in her handbag.

"It's a matter of taste, Miss. We cater for the general public. I'm sorry you——"

Terry shot over her shoulder, "You're sorry I don't like sewage?. . . Come on, Verna."

They emerged into Lower Regent Street, and walked towards Piccadilly Circus. Verna was the first to speak:

"Terry, you've pluck!"

"Let's go and have tea," was the only reply she received.

At the corner they waited for a lull in the traffic, and then crossed the Circus, ablaze already with electric signs. On the further side they made their way through the crowd towards Coventry Street, past the brilliance of the Pavilion blaring some super-revue.

"Look at the swine, gloating."

Two men, occupied with the photos of a leg-show plastering the entrance, turned at Terry's comment. Verna heard:

"Damned cheek!"

"No. Bit of bunk . . . What, what?"

Terry found them following, and flew out with:

"Get back to your swill-trough!"

It startled them. They stopped sheepishly, and then turned

back. Terry and Verna walked on.

"Terry, you're in form."

"I'm in a temper. . . . Here, this'll do."

They entered the restaurant. It was thronged. Terry surveyed:

"Phew, what a fug! . . . Upstairs."

On the floor above there was more room. They chose a table apart in a corner, sat down, and ordered tea. Terry looked about her, then resumed:

"'The general public'! . . . The damn-fool public!"

"Hold on, Terry. They'll hear."

"Do 'em good. That smug ape was probably right—they cater for that sniggering crowd."

Verna endeavoured to conciliate:

"I know. That sniggering irritates."

Terry opened her handbag, and began attending to her face:

"I'm all red and flushed."

"I suppose I'm more used to it," Verna said unwisely.

"Used to what?"

"All that sort of thing."

"Well, I refuse to get used to it!" Something in the background caught Terry's eye. "One can't get used to—*that*. . . . Look at it! . . . Good heavens, one can't even have tea . . ."

Verna screwed round. Through the windows, across Coventry Street, there was an immense flood-lit poster of a man embracing an unclothed chorus-girl, with a bevy grinning round.

"Pretty loathsome," she commented.

Their tea arrived. Terry asked the waitress:

"Is the view included in the tea?"

The waitress looked:

"All right for 'er."

Terry's eyes followed her retreating figure:

"'All right for 'er'!"

"'General public' opinion, my dear."

Terry gave a grunt, and lapsed into silence, pouring out tea. Verna took her cup and stirred thoughtfully. She tried:

"I'm not unsympathetic, because I don't get worked up. I didn't mind coming out in the least. I'm glad we did."

Terry regarded her, between sips of tea; she was cooling down:

"You'd have stayed if you'd been alone?"

"I don't know . . . No, I think I'd have come out. Dirt's offensive."

"To an idealist, I suppose?"

Verna ignored the sarcasm, and considered.

"Dirt's a blare of Jazz across a Beethoven Sonata. Strips the romance off things. That's my reaction."

Terry sniffed:

"What's the 'reaction' of the 'General public'?"

"Purely animal, probably."

"Yours is purely mental? A shade higher? . . . Heavens, haven't you a *moral* sense?"

Verna was laughing.

"I don't get morally outraged."

"Give me a cigarette."

Verna produced her case. They lit up.

"If I ran off with somebody's husband?"

Verna inhaled thoughtfully at the proposition.

"That's not on a par with a dirty film."

"Indecency's not immoral, then?" Terry asked.

"Repugnant, more."

Terry indicated the flood-lit poster across Coventry Street:

"You *could* have been *that*." She was serious suddenly: "Why aren't you?"

"You're reducing it to the personal," Verna evaded.

"Not an answer, my dear."

Verna was colouring. She looked down at her plate. The other suggested:

"Repugnant to tired business-men?"

There was no reply to the cynicism. The waitress arrived with their bill. Terry paid and tipped her.

"Look here——"

Verna cut across her sharply: "All right, then, I've a moral sense, or I'd have been a show-girl. Do you mind leaving it alone?"

Terry relit her cigarette in a determined way.

"No, I don't think I will . . . What's up?"

Verna flared:

"Can't you be less persistent? You're tactful as a rule."

Terry studied her perplexedly, wondering what raw spot she had touched. Things had abruptly reversed themselves. It was Verna now.

"Sorry. Can't get you at all, my dear."

"I don't want you to get me. I'd sooner you didn't."

Terry said:

"Oh? . . . Come along, then."

She flicked some ash from her dress, and picked up her handbag.

Verna did not move, however. Terry replaced her handbag, crushed out her cigarette-end and leaned across:

"What on earth's wrong, Verna?"

The other's expression all in a moment softened.

"Oh, I don't know . . ." She raised her head. There was a distress in the violet eyes. "S—something's happened. . . ." She stuck, as though in doubt of continuing. "One's g—got to revise one's whole estimate of things—life, everything . . . You've never had to do it, Terry."

Terry waited, wondering what was coming. Verna glanced about her, and said jerkily:

"This is the wrong place altogether; but I'd better tell you, or—— Terry, I'm definitely—— I've decided definitely—something appallingly big."

"Yes?"

"I—I've finished with the pater, but I'll be a Catholic. Do you understand?... Only——"

"Verna, this is——"

"I thought it would be easy—the rest; but it's not. I went to Father Thornton yesterday . . . One's not allowed one's own views, apparently."

"Views?"

"He said the sixth commandment wasn't popular nowadays. I wasn't sure which it was, so he gave me a Catechism. Terry, it's childish . . . I don't mean the 'adultery' part."

"What—'Pictures' and things? 'Plays'? 'Books'?"

"Yes. They're forbidden, apparently."

"'Immodest' ones."

"I told him I preferred the word 'vulgar'. 'Immodesty''s appallingly Victorian."

"What did he say?"

"He sort of sounded me, and said I'd have to change my views."

"Well, naturally."

"I simply haven't the Catholic view."

Her tone was obstinate again.

"There isn't a Catholic 'view'," Terry said. "Things are modest or immodest."

"It cramps one's outlook. I've sufficient moral sense to keep straight without exactitudes of 'modesty' to go by."

"So have young men—who don't."

"Then, they're immoral. I'm not."

Terry put in quickly:

"Because they begin by gloating over inexactitudes called 'immodesty'."

Verna examined the table-cloth:

"Men are swine!"

"So chorus-girls without exactitudes discover."

It was becoming rather irrelevant.

"Louis'd never be a swine, with a thousand chorus-girls about," came warmly.

"Louis'd not be there," Terry answered.

"That's his Catholic training."

"Yes, the Sixth Commandment."

Verna made as if to reply, but instead subsided into silence.

She picked up a crumb, looked at it, and threw it away; then suddenly volunteered the information:

"Father Thornton wants me to go to Lourdes. In May."

"Lourdes?"

"I want to go as a Catholic."

"Oh? . . . Will he receive you by May?"

Verna did not answer the question. Instead:

"He says I've a streak of the rebellious in me still . . . Terry, he was nice, really. He called all this—gibbing at the feel of the harness. We talked horses in the end."

"Oh?" Terry was not quite satisfied. "Then, it's going to be all right?"

The unburdening of her soul seemed to have had its effect; for Verna looked up, smiling:

"It will be, I think. After a last kick or two."

Terry reminded her:

"You've had *one*, now."

A shade of anxiety returned:

"There'll be another next quarter."

"How?"

"When the allowance doesn't turn up."

Terry's forehead wrinkled:

"It's as bad as that?"

"I'm afraid so."

Verna's lips were twitching.

"Verna! Is it really?"

There was a swallowing sound.

"What? Everything?"

"Yes. They said so—if I did it."

The simple statement conveyed the realities of the situation. Terry waited, digesting it; and then laid her hand on the other's resting on the table:

"My dear, you're very, very splendid!"

"I'll not make a very splendid pauper," came whimsically.

Terry said stoutly:

"You'll stick to the staid companion, my dear—until——"

She stopped short, and asked:

"Does Louis know?"

Verna remained without answering, regarding her thoughtfully.

"Where is he—at the moment?"

"Paris," said Verna. She picked up her gloves and adjusted her hat. "Terry, do you mind if we cable him, now?"

.　　　.　　　.　　　.　　　.

They were walking a quarter of an hour later up Shaftesbury Avenue, past the Trocadero.

Across the road, a theatre queue was forming beneath an electric sign winking, "Unmarried Love"—with mechanical persistence. Beyond, a rival queue favoured, "Should Husbands Tell?" On this side, the Trocadero's windows exhibited cabaret photos of a dancing troupe.

They passed on.

Chapter Twelve

"What'll Louis do?" Terry asked.

"If he can, he'll come straight back," was Verna's confident answer. "He promised."

Their attention was arrested by a crowd further on, blocking the other pavement. There was something unusual happening, for people were crossing the road. A head, visible above the level of the rest, appeared to be the centre of attraction. They paused as they came opposite. It startled them both, when they recognised that head.

"Father Thornton! . . ."

Verna took Terry by the arm:

"What on earth——"

They crossed over quickly, and wedged their way into the crush.

It was certainly Father Thornton.

In the white light from an arc-lamp the monk was standing with his arms akimbo facing an infuriated man, who was shouting and gesticulating. The pavement round was littered with torn magazines. There were wide gaps in the disordered lines of illustrated papers adorning the shopfront behind.

"Yew pay for thees! . . . He has rueened the papers! . . . I loos my money!"

The monk was regarding him coolly, without moving. A weedy-looking young man had appeared cautiously from inside, watching from the entrance:

"Yer damned——"

The monk stepped up to him. The young man removed his person within. There was a nervous laugh from those nearby. The monk reached up, pulled down another magazine and held it up before the proprietor whose thick Jewish lips were protruded in speechless fury. It was open at the picture of a naked woman. There was a tearing sound as he ripped the pages across, before flinging it down to join its companions on the pavement.

"Now, send for the police."

The man stared at him, all in a moment subdued. The monk pulled down another paper exhibiting photos of a nudist colony, held it up also, tore and flung it down.

"Send for the police."

The man looked hesitatingly at the faces round, gaping in the white glare, and then back at the monk who appeared to be measuring something with his eye, and whose foot suddenly lifted. A stand of magazines was dispersed in a jumbled heap with a clatter of trestles on the pavement.

The monk took a pair of gloves from his overcoat pocket, and put them on slowly, with his eyes on the proprietor, whose hands were clenching and unclenching in impotent frenzy. As he walked off, a man in a slouch hat intercepted him, breathlessly:

"Excuse me, sir."

The man raised his hat, and drew out a pencil and note-book.

"Yes? Who are you?"

"The Daily——"

"Then, get away."

The monk turned his back on him and strode off in the direction of Charing Cross Road. The crowd stared after him, and then broke into jabbering groups. The proprietor's tongue loosened and he began vociferously apostrophising a rapidly dissolving audience. He was interrupted by the man in the slouch hat, with a request for particulars.

Verna and Terry found themselves staring at one another, on the edge of the pavement.

Chapter XIII

A T THE TOP of the companion-way a man, with an attaché case in his hand, was surveying the cliffs drawing near. Captain Vivien was surveying the man's back.

"It is your first sight, my friend, of the white walls of Dover."

As the bell for half-speed sounded, the man made a move, and descended the stairway. Captain Vivien waited for a moment on the upper deck before descending himself.

When the boat was alongside the harbour Captain Vivien was behind the man in the passenger queue for the gangway. The hat beneath his nose was probably of English make, and certainly quite new.

On the Dover platform, after the Customs' formalities were over, Captain Vivien stood lighting a cigarette. The porter behind him with his bags asked, "First-class, sir?" Captain Vivien ignored the question: "You will wait here one minute, while I buy newspapers."

He went to the bookstall and bought *The Illustrated London News* and the *Daily Mail,* and then stood, turning over the pages of the former, facing where the passengers from the Customs were filing through to the platform. He turned, a minute later, facing the Dover-London train, and continued to turn over the pages of *The Illustrated London News.* Then he walked across to the porter.

"First-class, sir?"

"I will choose my carriage. I am particular with whom I travel. It is a habit."

In the corner of a first-class compartment, facing the engine, Captain Vivien composed himself for sleep, whilst the man with the new hat was placing the same on the rack by his attaché case, and removing his overcoat. He lit a cigarette, steadying himself to the swaying of the train, and then manœuvred past Captain Vivien's legs into the corridor, and disappeared.

Captain Vivien's eyes opened. He watched the corridor for a moment, then rose, sniffed at the cloud of cigarette-smoke, reached down the man's hat from the rack, examined the inside, and put it back. Without disarranging the overcoat on the seat, which was also new-looking and of grey material, he looked at the inside of the collar, murmuring to himself: "You are an interesting man . . . to buy an English coat in Moscow and an English hat in Berlin . . . where you stop on the way. . . . It is nice to have so much money—for the double price. . . . It is better, however, that you smoke English cigarettes; it is more harmonious."

Captain Vivien was breathing regularly with his mouth slightly open when the man re-entered the compartment, and resumed his seat in the further corner, also facing the engine. After watching the landscape gliding by for a while, the man took down his attaché case from the rack, unlocked it, and found a small red-bound book inside. He placed the attaché case on the seat, between them, and began to read. Captain Vivien, heavily asleep, observed that it was a dictionary of some kind.

Chapter Thirteen

Half way to London, the man put down the dictionary on the seat. Captain Vivien, still heavily asleep, saw *Russian-English* on the cover.

The man stretched, and glanced at his travelling companion; then he took out of the attaché case what appeared to be a number of letters with an india-rubber band round, which he removed. He selected some typed sheets fastened together with a wire clip, replaced the band round the rest, returned them to the case, and became absorbed in whatever the sheets contained.

Captain Vivien watched, and became most intrigued. The fingers of the man's free hand were mechanically playing with, twisting and curling something totally invisible beneath his chin. The man suddenly awoke to the fact and dropped his hand, amused at himself. Captain Vivien observed little tufts of hair left by the razor in the cleft of his chin.

He was still absorbed, when Captain Vivien woke up gruntingly. At the sound there was an instinctive movement of the hand holding the sheets. The man looked up for a moment. He became, however, once more engrossed. Captain Vivien waited until the last page had been turned over.

"You will excuse me?"

The man made an acquiescent sound, as Captain Vivien reached up to his bag half way along the rack, and said "Damn!" as he inserted the wrong key in the lock. There was an interval during which he stood feeling amongst the coins in his pocket for another, with his head turned nearer and his eyes searching swiftly that last page. The head beneath him did not move. He found the right key, with an "Ah!" opened and searched the bag with his hand, and produced a pipe and tobacco pouch, relocked the bag, sat down again, and filled the pipe. Before closing the tobacco pouch, which was bulky and had a curious little round hole in the centre, he inserted his fingers again, and then manœuvred it cautiously with the hole facing the man's profile. . . . An almost inaudible click was covered by the noise of the train. Captain Vivien closed and placed the pouch in his pocket, lit his pipe, slipped on his gloves, and picked up the *Illustrated London News*.

A minute later the first finger of his right glove, which had an inconspicuous, minute point at the tip, was writing on the outside margin of a page a sentence in inverted commas, and then the words: "From K. to R. of the Committee"; also a telephone number.

After a few minutes perusal of the *Illustrated London News*, Captain Vivien put it behind his back, and found a cablegram in his breast-pocket, which he read, smiling. It ran: "Have done the big thing remember your promise all my love Verna". The cablegram was returned to his pocket. On a telegram form which he took from his note-case, he then wrote with an ordinary pencil: "Have returned but perhaps am detained shall come to you very happy I love you Louis". He folded the form and inserted it within his glove.

The outer suburbs of London were flying by. He looked at the man again, who was now leaning forward staring intently through the window. The light was on his face, emphasizing the heavy projection of bone above the beady eyes, the brutal receding forehead beneath wiry straight hair awkwardly parted, and the unpleasing curl of the protruding underlip.

Captain Vivien removed his eyes; they fell on the unopened *Daily Mail*. He picked it up and scanned the headlines. At the centre page his attention was suddenly riveted: "Scene in Shaftesbury Avenue"—"Monk's violent action". He read beneath: "An amazing scene was witnessed last night in Shaftesbury Avenue, when the Roman Catholic monk, Father Anselm Thornton . . ."

Chapter Thirteen

He reached the bottom of the column as the train slowed down into the London terminus, folded the paper thoughtfully, rose and placed it with the *Illustrated London News* in his bag, glanced at the man, who was putting on his hat and overcoat, and extracted the telegram from his glove.

To the porter who had secured his baggage, he said, when they were on the platform: "You will find me a taxi very quickly, if you please," and, when it drew up to the pavement a minute later: "You will send this telegram for me? Thank you. And you will take five shillings." "Yessir . . . Very good, sir. Much obliged . . . Thank you, sir." The porter put the baggage inside, touched his cap three times, and went off with the telegram.

To the taxi-man Captain Vivien said: "We will wait one moment." He stepped inside, sat down, and watched his companion of the first-class compartment standing further down the platform, with an ungainly forward slouch, explaining something to a porter who was scratching his head, with his cap pushed back. The porter disappeared inside the luggage-van, emerged, pulling with him a large metal-bound box, found a trolley on which he heaved it, and then beckoned the owner to follow. Captain Vivien put his head out: "You will follow the taxi into which the big box goes . . . You see?" The taxi-man screwed round at him, and then looked in the direction indicated. "And it will be double the fare, if we stop where the big box stops . . . You understand?" The taxi-man screwed round again, had a good look at him, said, "Righto, sir . . . Thank you," and then riveted his attention on proceedings ahead.

The taxi with the box took a West-end direction from the station. The second taxi followed doggedly for some minutes, fifty yards behind, to be held up at the end of Piccadilly while the first was crossing the Circus. Captain Vivien said: "Damn," put his head out of the window and called, "See the way which he takes!" The driver turned with a wink: "Dontcher worry—I got 'im, sir." A moment later Captain Vivien found himself driven across the Circus, and sharply to the left, up to the portico of a resplendent hotel, disappearing into which were the man and his box.

In the same resplendent hotel, ten minutes later, Captain Vivien was pacing up and down a room on the third floor, with the *Illustrated London News* lying open near the telephone. He went to the door suddenly and locked it; then came back muttering to himself:

"It is a very great gamble...."

His eyes rested on the paper. He looked at the telephone number which he had written in the margin.

"It is a very great gamble...."

Then he picked up the receiver and asked for the Exchange....

"Number, please."

He gave it and waited.

After a while he heard the receiver at the other end being lifted. A voice with a pronounced accent asked:

"Yes?... Who is that?"

Captain Vivien delayed a moment, before saying gutturally:

"Yes?... But, I cannot hear."

There was some tapping. The voice asked again:

"Who are you?"

"Yes?... Yes, I am speaking to you from the hotel. I have come."

The voice asked tentatively:

"Then, it is Roslavl?"

Captain Vivien became taut. He said quickly:

"Karenov, you will listen . . . Yes, it is Roslavl. I have come, but it has been difficult. . . . You are alone?"

"Yes. I am alone."

Captain Vivien said in a nervous tone:

"I am followed to the hotel . . . You hear me, Karenov?"

There was a pause.

"How—— But, it is not so?"

Captain Vivien's fist thumped the table:

"I am saying what is true. I do not understand, because I have shaved the beard, and I have English clothes. But, there is a man of the Intelligence Service in the train with me, who follows me here, and who has a room in the hotel which is near from my room."

He heard a sucking sound. And then a grunt.

"That is bad."

There was another grunt.

"It will be better for you to go from the hotel immediately."

Captain Vivien assumed irritation:

"I am not a fool that I stay here."

The other appeared to be thinking. The voice said after an interval:

"You will listen, Roslavl . . . You will not come to me, yet. I do not like it that you are watched."

"I understand. But, you will tell me what you wish that I do?"

"It is not safe, that we are together—you understand?"

"No, I do not come to you. But, what do you wish that I do?"

He risked it: "In the letter you do not explain enough."

The voice came emphatically:

"I do not wish that you do anything. The Committee are fools that they send you. . . . But, you have the Commission, and I do not interfere."

Captain Vivien retorted sharply:

"I have the Commission because the Committee are not fools; so you will assist me, Karenov."

"I give you the place of the monk, where he lives. But, I do not assist you more, because it is dangerous what you do, and I do not wish that I am associated."

Captain Vivien's fingers had closed tightly. His lips framed a disgruntled:

"It is enough that I have the Commission——" He was suddenly alert to the other giving him an address . . .

"Yes? . . . Yes, I have it. I write it." He kept silent, as though doing so. Then: "Karenov, there is about a monk in the English newspaper of this morning——"

The voice cut in sharply: "Yes, it is the same man. Do you not see his name? . . . Roslavl, you do not come, but you speak to me only by telephone. You understand?"

"Yes. I am not stupid . . . I say goodbye to you."

He put back the receiver with a bang, to convey irritation; then went to the door and unlocked it. His hand went mechanically to his pocket. It was trembling a little. He took out his case, and lit a cigarette slowly.

Then remained standing there—rigid.

CHAPTER XIV

THE MONK WAS at his desk with his letters, when the tap came on the door and a lay-brother entered:

"Captain Vivien to see you, Father."

The monk laid down his pen.

"Captain Vivien?"

He gathered the sheets before him together.

"Ask him to come up."

The lay-brother disappeared. The monk rose, looked at the clock which informed him that it was a quarter to ten, went to the fire, kicked a coal into position and waited, until he heard the sound of foot-steps along the corridor outside. A familiar figure appeared in the doorway.

"Good morning, my Padre. I see you first, before I see Verna."

The monk eyed him up and down:

"How do you do, *amico mio*. This is very nice."

He betrayed no surprise, though Louis usually gave warning; but pulled up a chair, and sat him down.

"I may smoke here? Thank you."

The monk sat down himself, and watched him lighting up.

"Padre, I have a cablegram from Verna two days ago in Paris; so I come back yesterday. It is the big thing. You have done this?"

The monk smiled:

"Very little. She came and told me."

Captain Vivien's eyes were searching him.

"And she is very happy?"

"Now. Yes," said the monk.

"Now?"

"There was something—— She'll tell you."

Captain Vivien looked anxious for a moment:

"But, it is all right?"

"Absolutely."

The monk swung round, reached for a pile of letters on his desk, and picked out a blue envelope.

"That's from her, this morning. It's rather interesting. Read it."

The other took the envelope, extracted the letter, and began to read. Half way through he looked up:

"That is strange . . . I have seen about it in the newspaper yesterday."

"No doubt. Go on."

Captain Vivien read aloud:

"'. . . You didn't know that Terry and I were watching. I think it must have been by some extraordinary providence that we were in Shaftesbury Avenue at the time. I don't know why; but it gave me a sort of moral jolt. Something clicked in me last night.

"'I tried to argue against your violence; but I was arguing against myself. You must have thought me exceedingly obstinate over my "views"; you see, I was never brought up to regard these things in the moral light. I've always judged them by good taste or art, or what was sacred to me personally. I'd never related them to a moral law. The word "sin" meant very little.

"'I saw it, before I fell asleep. That paper shop was sin incarnate; or you couldn't have done it? Thank you, dear Father; because it helped . . .'"

The monk said: "Go on."

Louis read:

Chapter Fourteen

"'P.S. May I begin instructions now? P.P.S. Two corollaries. (a) I've suddenly found that I believe in a *real* Devil, without any difficulty. Louis' Devil. (b) I'm enormously happy. I've a sense for the first time of being completely in tune with Louis and you and Terry.'"

Captain Vivien looked up, smiling radiantly. He returned the letter to the monk:

"I have told Verna in Richmond Park, before I went away, what you have said to me."

"What was that?"

"I must be patient, because she has a heart of gold. I am glad that I have waited—for the big thing to happen. . . . You will begin the instructions with her?"

"Straight away, my Louis."

"Because she is everything in the good God's world to me."

He looked away through the window. His expression changed suddenly. The monk asked:

"You've something to tell me, haven't you? Why haven't you gone to Verna first?"

Captain Vivien rose, and began to walk about.

"Well?"

He stopped and looked at the monk.

"My Padre, you will have to be very careful."

The other screwed round.

"How?"

"No, I do not mean the paper-shop. Padre, who is Roslavl?"

The monk's forehead wrinkled.

"Roslavl?"

"It is the name of a man who comes to England yesterday. A man who comes from Russia."

"Oh?"

"Padre, you will think, if you please; because the brain of the Intelligence Service is tired of wondering why a man called

145

Roslavl hates an English monk so very much."

"Indeed? As far as the English monk can recollect, he has never heard the name in his life."

"He has not known you in England, because I do not think he has been in England before. But you have been in Russia— in Archangel—with the British Force, when that ugly thing has happened."

"Yes. For a few weeks."

"Then I think it is in those few weeks that the Russian man, Roslavl, has met you."

"Why should he have met me, at all?"

"I have deduced it, because I have to explain to myself; something has happened that he hates you."

The monk leaned back and pondered the matter.

"A Russian? Who hates me? Who has met me? Roslavl? . . . I met a good many Russians during those weeks . . . Hates me?"

Captain Vivien's finger-tips met:

"A man who comes a long way to do a thing which is not safe for himself, has always a strong motive. If he is a Russian, who has a Commission from a Committee for his work, and if his work is with an English monk, who is the Padre Thornton, and if Karenov is not agreed, because the work is dangerous—then it is not difficult to guess for what the man Roslavl comes to England, and that he has personal reasons. It is not dangerous to do something good; it is dangerous to do something bad; but Roslavl takes the risk because he hates the English Padre. It is very simple, is it not?" The monk was watching him now, keenly.

"And where did you get all this?"

"It is a habit of the Intelligence Service. But I do not tell you how. You do not believe?"

The monk picked up a pen, played with it, and put it down again.

"Believe? What? . . . That some madman——"

"But I do not think he is a madman," the other interrupted. "He is a devil, and he is not a stranger to you. Padre, you will think again, please. You have made an enemy in Russia? You have had a quarrel?"

"I had barely a week in Archangel—before that happening in the forest; and then a month in hospital. I made no enemies. The White officers were friendly, all of them."

Captain Vivien shook his head:

"Roslavl would not have been an officer. He is rough, brutal—from the scum, I think."

The monk affirmed:

"I never met that type. Except in the Red Recruits."

"The Red Recruits?"

"Red prisoners were allowed to enlist with the British."

Captain Vivien paused.

"They were friendly? The Red Recruits?"

"Quite . . . Only——"

The monk suddenly rose and crossed the room to a bureau of drawers.

"Only what? . . . You have remembered something?"

He unlocked the top drawer, searched inside, and returned with a package in his hand.

"Who were the men who crucified Major Rodney in the forest of Archangel, and who did not succeed in killing you?"

The monk sat down and untied the package: "I may be able to tell you in a minute." It contained some letters and a note-book. He opened the note-book, and began turning over the leaves: "They were Red prisoners who tried to enlist with us, and whom I failed in the Medical examination. I've an idea their names are here."

Captain Vivien watched.

"And that is——"

"A note-book of Major Rodney's, which I kept."

The monk's finger was on a list of names handwritten down a page, under a date in 1919. He studied them, and then handed the note-book to Captain Vivien, with:

"There are crosses against six names out of those twenty. Major Rodney apparently drafted in fourteen. The six with the crosses would be the ones I failed, and therefore whom he refused to draft in."

The other examined the list closely. He raised his head:

"Padre, I am glad you have kept this."

"It's interesting, certainly."

"It is interesting that one of the six men has the name—Roslavl. Now, you will think again, please, of the faces of those men, if you can remember them?"

The answer came decidedly:

"Only one. Their leader's. It was the kind of face one doesn't forget."

"You could describe it?"

"I could draw it, roughly, I think."

The monk turned round to his desk, took a pen and a sheet of paper. Captain Vivien watched over his shoulder, as the other drew a profile with a receding forehead and an abnormal projection of bone over the eyes. The pen hesitated over the nose, but not over the mouth, which appeared with a protruding, curling underlip, and a beard beneath. He put down the pen with: "The eyes were small; out of proportion. Black, I expect."

Captain Vivien produced from a note-case, and laid down beside the drawing, a snap-shot of a man's side-face against the blurred outline of a railway-carriage window. The monk stared at it.

"Is that Roslavl?"

"That is the man Roslavl, who is now in London. Put your hand over the beard which you have drawn."

The monk did so.

Chapter Fourteen

"You have drawn Roslavl very well, my Padre."

The monk fingered the photograph ponderingly. He turned and looked up. Their eyes met.

"So you understand, now? . . . If I ask you why those six men do that ugly thing with you and Major Rodney, what is the answer that you give?"

"That you're asking me a difficult question."

"But there was a motive?" Captain Vivien persisted.

"Oh yes. Revenge, according to G.H.Q. Red traitors. Similar things had happened before."

"Revenge? Because you have not drafted them in?"

"Partly," said the monk. "They were probably looters. We deprived them of a favourable opportunity."

"But it does not explain everything?"

"The elaborate brutality in the forest? No, not quite."

Captain Vivien considered.

"It was planned, you think, very carefully?"

"They could have shot us down in the timber-yard, where they trapped us. I can remember wondering at the time why they didn't. My Louis, if you ask me why they preferred to risk capture after escaping, for the sole purpose of executing a carefully calculated torture on two British officers, who had merely refused to draft them in—well, I've only one answer. You asked me for the motive?"

"I have asked you, because it is important."

"Then—Red hate. And you cannot analyse Red hate. It's beyond analysis."

"I see . . . Because it is beyond what is human?"

The monk said slowly:

"If ever Satan walked this earth, he was in the forest of Archangel that night."

Captain Vivien remained silent. He began pacing about again, with his forehead furrowing.

"So the leader of those six men, Roslavl—somehow he finds out that the British Medical Officer, who is fixed to the tree to die of exposure in the forest—— Yes, somehow he finds out. . . . It is that Karenov reports from England to the Committee in Russia about the English Padre Thornton? Who speaks against Bolshevism?—It is difficult, this— How does Roslavl——"

"May I help?" the monk put in.

The other stood still.

"Somebody, a journalist, I suppose, got hold fairly accurately of the main facts of the story; it appeared in the newspapers here."

Captain Vivien came nearer:

"Indeed? While I am in Paris?"

"A few weeks ago."

"And they have said that the Padre Thornton is the man who was brought back from the forest?"

"They made the story out of that," said the monk.

Captain Vivien smiled:

"Thank you. It is not difficult now. It is easy."

The monk was not quite so sure:

"He got it from Karenov? How?"

"Because Roslavl is upon the Committee also."

The monk regarded him questioningly.

"Is that guess-work?"

"No. It is a habit of the Intelligence Service."

Captain Vivien was feeling for his cigarette-case. His hand returned empty from his pocket. He went to his overcoat, laid on a chair against the further wall, and picked it up—to be suddenly arrested by a shaving-mirror hung above. The overcoat was lowered slowly. The monk saw him glance round at the window opposite, and then stand away a little to the side. "My Padre, because you hang your mirror in the right place, I can tell you now the rest of that story which began on that night in the forest of Archangel."

The monk frowned perplexedly. He stood up, went across to the mirror and studied it, mystified.

"You do not see the rest of the story from there. But, in a minute, you shall. I will tell you."

He spoke quickly and concentratedly:

"The leader, Roslavl, who has left the Medical Officer in the forest to die with his friend whom they have crucified—Roslavl succeeds so that he crosses the frontier to the Reds. He is a brute; but he is a clever brute, who works his way up. And so he is now upon the Red Committee in Moscow which sends agents from Russia; of whom Karenov is one, in England. It is in a letter, or in a report, of Karenov to the Committee that there is contained the newspaper story of the Padre Thornton, who works in England against Bolshevism; so Roslavl knows that the wolves did not find the Medical Officer for food in the forest that night so long ago. It is very—provoking for Roslavl, is it not? . . . My Padre, you have said Red hate, it is beyond analysis; and I am agreed with you. I have asked you to be very careful, because it is as relentless as the Devil himself, and because it follows you like the Devil himself. . . . So you will please not go near to the window. . . . But, you will like to see the rest of the story?" Captain Vivien stood him at an angle before the shaving-mirror, and pointed.

The monk saw the reflection of the window behind, and the opposite pavement of the street outside. Framed in the circle of the mirror, a man in a grey overcoat was standing there in the sunlight, studying the building before him.

The monk remained still, watching.

"So that's—Roslavl."

Captain Vivien remarked:

"It is careless that he buys an English overcoat in Moscow."

CHAPTER XV

IN THE DRAWING-ROOM of the Bayswater flat, Verna, taking
a telephone call, lifted the receiver to hear a familiar voice
at the other end.

"Louis!"

"My Verna, I make two thousand apologies. You have received my telegram yesterday?"

"Yes. What's been happening?"

He replied:

"Yesterday, it is Foreign Affairs. This morning, it is the
Church of God. The Intelligence Service——"

"——doesn't answer questions. Where are you speaking
from?"

"From the room of this man with whom you are 'in tune'."

"What?"

She caught a second voice in the background, and a crin-
kling of paper. Louis' voice resumed:

"The incriminating evidence, it is in your own handwriting.
I read it to you: 'I have a sense for the first time of being completely in tune with Louis and you and Terry'. In future, you
will please only be completely in tune with one man."

She replied:

"Tell the Church of God not to cast my pearls before the
Unintelligence Service. Why are you ringing me up? Why don't
you come along? It's eleven already."

"Because I wait here until there is a movement in Foreign

affairs."

"Don't be cryptic."

"Meanwhile I occupy myself by listening to my Verna's voice, while I study the glass."

"The glass? . . . Are you going lightheaded, Louis?"

"It is the sound of your voice . . . But I think . . . Yes . . . That is good . . . There is a local depression, which moves . . . That is very good. So I come along now in a taxi——"

"Wait a minute. Terry's butting in."

Terry had entered. She took the receiver from Verna's hand and quoted at the mouthpiece: "'Oh joy, oh rapture unforeseen. The clouded sky is now serene . . .'" Verna pulled her away and retrieved the receiver:

"Louis, if you're not here immediately, Terry acts as proxy."

Louis replied hastily:

"That is the ultimatum? I come at once—— No, there is a little domestic affair. I am with you at twelve o'clock."

"Right. The ultimatum expires at midday."

Verna hung up the receiver, smiling.

His ring came at five minutes to the hour.

.   .   .   .   .

In the drawing-room, after lunch, when the coffee-cups had been removed, Terry stood up, straightened herself and said primly:

"Let us all three walk round Kensington Gardens?"

Captain Vivien's eyes met Verna's.

"Let us all three go to the National Gallery?"

There was no response.

"Let us all three discuss the political situation?"

Verna picked up a newspaper.

Terry wandered to the window.

"Let us all three——"

She was seized by the two of them, propelled towards the door and pushed out. The door was closed after her. From the other side came a rendering of the Wedding March. After which Terry retired to her room.

They remained regarding each other rather shyly; until Louis took her face between his hands:

"My Verna."

He kissed her. She said rather breathlessly:

"You're an absolute dear to have come. Did you mind the cablegram?"

"I would come to you from all round the world."

He led her by the hand to the sofa. They sat with hands clasped like two children. She told him:

"I can hardly believe, yet."

"And what?"

"That it's really happened."

He answered:

"I have known always—somehow it will happen. You remember? Richmond Park?"

"Could I forget it? I called you cruel."

"I have not understood what you have done, until this morning. Until the Padre has told me."

Verna laid her hands on his shoulders:

"You know, then? I've nothing? I'll be living on Terry now."

"For a little while only."

She put her hand over his mouth:

"Louis, I know what you're going to say. But you're not to say it, yet."

He removed her hand and kissed it:

"That is your wicked pride."

"I've not much left. It's not that. I've to prove myself, Louis."

"To prove yourself?"

"That it's the Faith, and not just you."

Chapter Fifteen

He saw what she meant.

"Now, you will listen, please. It is very simple. Next year in the Spring, you are received into the Church; I have asked the Padre, and he agrees—so you will be very good with the instructions? Afterwards we are all very happy because you are a Catholic; so we make the Pilgrimage in May and say thank you to our Lady of Lourdes, because I have asked her for the big thing to happen——"

"You wanted me to go to Lourdes. You remember? On the boat?"

He nodded, smiling:

"And when we come back, Louis says to himself that he is getting old——"

"And Verna says he's absurd. Yes?"

"And that the time has come when he—what do you say?"

"Settles down into a contented old age. Yes?"

"So he resigns from the Intelligence Service of France."

"Yes?"

"And lives in the old-fashioned house in the country which he has found in the *Illustrated London News*, and about which he telephones to the agent this morning."

"Louis! . . . Not really?" she exclaimed.

"Because it is near to London, when, perhaps, he works at Scotland Yard."

"Louis!"

"And so he lives there amongst the birds and the trees and the flowers."

Louis paused.

"It is a very wonderful idea?"

He pulled her nose.

She asked:

"Is that the Great Romance?"

He suddenly got up:

"You will excuse me? I may use the telephone?"

"Y—yes. Of course."

He went to the table on which it was standing, took up the receiver, listened, and then gave a number and waited. "Hullo. It is the House Agents'?. . . Captain Vivien speaking. You will keep the house of which I speak to you this morning. Tomorrow I will go down there to see it."

He listened, saying "Yes?" at times, and finally: "That is very good. Your agent will have the keys? I will be there at twelve o'clock."

He hung up the receiver, and went back to the sofa.

Verna was endeavouring to look horrified:

"Louis, what *are* you doing?"

"Tomorrow we go to see the house," he stated.

"It would be lovely." She assumed inapprehension. "But—— We?"

She found her hand being taken, and something being slipped on her finger. He announced:

"It is proper that we are engaged before we see the house."

Verna looked at the ring, and then slowly up into his face.

She laid her hands on the lapels of his coat. Her eyes were brimming. She shook her head, unable for the moment to speak. The tears were running down her cheeks:

"I—it's just happiness, Louis."

He put his arms round her, and drew her to himself:

"You will cry upon my coat, so that I will take away some of you with me."

She stayed with her face hidden against him; then drew his head down, and lifted her lips to his.

"Louis, why are you so good to me?"

"Am I good, because I love you?"

"I——I wanted to be just a humble penitent, for a time."

"You did not want—this?"

She laughed softly, and nestled closer.

"Do you know, I was afraid yesterday?"

"Afraid? Why?"

"I think it was having to wait; or the telegram. It suggested all sorts of horrible possibilities."

"It was a very clumsy telegram."

There was a sigh:

"Am I never to know what you're doing? Even when——"

She stopped short.

"You will say it, please," he commanded.

"Even when we're—— Louis, I can't. You've not asked me properly yet."

"That is very forgetful of the Intelligence Service. . . . If you please, will you marry me?"

The sharp ring of the telephone interrupted them. Verna sat up:

"It would, right in the middle of a proposal. . . . Sorry. Do you mind?" She went to the table, pulling him by the hand with her, and took the call. After listening for a moment, she turned:

"It's Father Thornton—'terribly sorry', etcetera. Would you speak with him alone?"

"I apologise," he said. "But I have asked him."

She handed him the receiver, with: "I'll be in the next room. Call me," and went out, closing the door behind her.

Captain Vivien spoke at the mouthpiece:

"Yes, Padre, I am alone."

He heard from the other end:

"I'm sorry; but you told me to."

He asked:

"So he is back again?"

"Same spot."

Captain Vivien frowned to himself:

"He can see from there the two doors . . . Yes . . . He just waits."

"Evidently," came the monk's voice. "Am I supposed to wait, as well?"

"I have told you."

"I've to catch a train at five. Victoria."

"Then you please will not catch that train."

There was an interval. The other's voice came:

"Aren't we exaggerating? The danger?"

"We are not. That man intends to kill you when he has the very first opportunity."

"Um . . . Well, there's a plain-clothes man."

"There is a plain-clothes man tomorrow morning. But plain-clothes men cannot prevent these things."

Another silence. The monk asked:

"How long's this going to last?"

"Perhaps for a few days. He will be very patient."

"Am I to be cooped up until—— Look here, my Louis, I've engagements, every day."

"If you are wise you will postpone them."

"What about the audiences? Sorry. I can't . . . They're in London. I'll take taxis."

"There is no guarantee for you, if you leave the house, Padre. Do you understand? He acts with a knife as well—because he is a Russian. And he is a fanatic; so he is prepared to be caught. And there is no evidence upon which he can be arrested to prevent him. You understand?"

"Perfectly. I'll take every reasonable precaution."

"You are obstinate, then?"

"Yes. I'm sorry, but——"

Captain Vivien banged the receiver down.

Verna must have heard it; for the door opened with: "You're an awful time." She came in:

"Is—— Louis, what's up?"

She stared at him.

"My dear Louis, you're all red. . . . What's happened?"

Captain Vivien was pacing about, fuming to himself.

"This isn't a bit like the Intelligence Service. . . . You're angry."

He stopped. His face suddenly softened.

"I am sorry, my Verna. I am very rude."

"Tell me, quietly—what's happened?"

"I cannot tell you . . . But it is necessary that I go to Scotland Yard—and that I am at Victoria Station, before it is five o'clock."

"Louis! . . . Today?"

He glanced at his wrist-watch:

"There will be a taxi in the Bayswater Road?"

"There's a Garage close by. But—— Shall I phone?"

"Please, now."

While she was doing so, Captain Vivien went into the hall, put on his overcoat, and came back with his hat and gloves in his hand. He waited until Verna put down the receiver:

"It's coming now . . . Louis, I'm frightened . . . Is there——"

"No, no, no. There is not danger—for me."

Her look of relief was only momentary.

"Is Father Thornton—— There was something wrong this morning, wasn't there? . . . Louis, you're worried."

He did not reply, but took her in his arms and kissed her:

"My beloved, tomorrow I come here, and we go to see the house."

He walked out quickly, without looking back.

Verna waited until she heard the click of the hall-door.

She stood for a moment with her hand to her cheek. Then went to a room across the passage and tapped: "Terry!"

Chapter XVI

As the Five p.m. from Victoria ran into Windern Station, a chauffeur in livery emerged from the waiting-room to take up his position on the platform under a lamp.

A carriage-door opened as the train came to a stand-still, and the monk stepped out. The chauffeur came up and touched his cap:

"Good evening, Father."

"Evening, Stanley."

The chauffeur took a suit-case from the monk, and led the way, through the booking-office, outside. The monk followed leisurely. While giving up his ticket, he glanced down the platform. He saw in the lamplight a figure step out of a carriage half-way down. He remembered afterwards seeing a carriage-door at the extreme end of the train slightly open.

Outside, in the road, he found the chauffeur holding open the door of the car. The monk put his head in and looked at the clock. It was five minutes past six.

"I'm going to walk, Stanley."

"Walk, Father?"

"Exercise. If you'll give the suit-case a lift."

"Two miles to Hendringham. Dark night, Father."

"Carry on. I know the way."

"Very good, Father."

Chapter Sixteen

The chauffeur hesitated for a moment, and then stepped inside.

The monk started off down the road to the left. A minute later the car passed him, gathering speed. Hedges and trees on in front rose in ghostly array, caught by the headlights before they swept round a bend to the right. Above him the train thundered by, and on into the night.

Beyond the bend, his eyes, growing accustomed to the dark, made out the straight line of the road ahead. He walked steadily on, through the now unbroken silence of the Sussex night. After a quarter of a mile he passed the lighted windows of a cottage, slightly quickening his pace as he crossed the patch of yellow on the road.

A hundred yards on he stopped abruptly, struck a match, held it before his face as though lighting a cigarette, and listened. From somewhere behind him a faintly audible sound of feet on the hard surface ceased also. He blew out the match and looked back. In the darkness beyond the yellow patch nothing was visible. A dog, barking in the distance, accentuated the stillness.

He went on.

After a short distance he looked back again, but without altering his pace. A figure was crossing the patch of light, on the left side of the road. The monk veered from the centre, keeping near to the hedge on the right. By slightly varying his step at intervals, he could catch the steady beat of feet behind.

He was straining his eyes ahead, when the headlights of a car came swinging round a corner from a side-road. The oncoming dazzle drove him close up to the ditch. As the car passed he shielded his eyes, and then turned swiftly. For a brief moment the figure behind was revealed in the glare— with a hand in an overcoat pocket.

The monk strode on.

The feet behind him were quickening as he reached the side-road to the right, from which the car had come. He made round the corner, scrambled up a turf bank, and thrust himself, back first, heedless of thorns, against the hedge.

The feet were nearing hurriedly now—in a way that told him his turn to the right had been seen. He waited, taut, with nerves tuned up to the peril. The man's pace slackened as he reached the corner . . .

The monk experienced a curious flash of recognition as Roslavl stood beneath him five yards away with a raised revolver, breathing quickly and searching about with the muzzle. For, in the forest of Archangel, seven years ago, Roslavl had stood in much the same way, following him with a revolver. There was no intention of failing this time; momentarily puzzled, though the man was, at not finding him within range.

The monk calculated swiftly. The revolver, by its outline, was six-chambered. Discovery at close quarters meant certain death. He could not remain cramped up for long without some sound betraying him in the stillness; and he doubted whether he was invisible . . . He knew his own strength. It was the revolver . . . Already Roslavl understood that he was somewhere in the shelter of the hedge. The levelled muzzle was searching every yard of it, further on, and then slowly nearer, approaching every second . . .

The monk landed on him just in time.

They fell together heavily on the road, with a bullet whistling upwards to the stars. The impact and explosion left them dazed; but only for a moment. The monk felt the muzzle being tugged from his grip; for the other had the butt. He let go and secured his wrist, twisting the arm down until the savage animal beneath him was snarling with pain. Without moving his weight, he worked his knee on to the wrist, unlocked the fingers, removed the revolver, and flung it into the darkness over the hedge.

Then he stood up, and contemplated that thwarted, maddened figure on the road.

"Get up!"

Roslavl did so; very slowly.

The monk heard the hiss of his breath, and mutterings in Russian. His hand was fumbling.

"Leave that knife!"

The hand continued to move.

"You——"

The monk caught a glint in the dark, as the other came at him with his hand upraised. He marked the black slits gleaming for his life, and then struck with his full length and strength . . . The knife came down on his shoulder, piercing the cloth of his coat. The clink of it on the road and a dull thud came simultaneously.

He gave himself time to recover his breath; then picked up the knife, looked at it, walked to the bank, stuck it in the earth, and drove it in with his heel out of sight.

He came back and stooped over the prostrate figure, lying there with face upturned.

"Padre, that was very good."

The monk started at the voice, and looked up. Another figure was standing there in black outline, looking on. He answered, after his first surprise:

"I couldn't wait for a week. It had to be settled—this."

He began examining the unconscious man, lifting the head and feeling with his fingers.

"Did you happen to see how he dropped?"

"He has not fallen on his head—no."

The head seemed all right.

"Give us a hand, Louis."

Between them they lifted Roslavl and carried him to the side, laying him against the bank. They searched his person, but found no further weapons.

"You were on that train?" the monk asked.

"Indeed, yes."

"You saw—all this?"

"I have him covered—from over there . . . After the cottage, it becomes exciting. So I run."

Captain Vivien showed a small-pattern revolver, and slipped it back into his overcoat pocket apologetically:

"I cannot fire, because you are somewhere in the dark. However, it is perhaps better—like this."

"Louis, you're a brick. I'm sorry I've given you all this bother . . . What are we going to do? I'm supposed to be on the way to Hendringham."

Captain Vivien studied the still figure between them, and then bent over. When he rose again, Roslavl was handcuffed. He asked the monk:

"You think he will be conscious? Soon?"

"Any time."

"Then you may go to Hendringham."

The monk did not move.

"There is no need for you now, Padre."

He asked:

"What'll you do? Take him back to London?"

"Indeed, yes."

"By yourself?"

"To the Windern Police-station. Why not? He is handcuffed. I have a revolver."

The monk appeared to be thinking.

"He'll go through the ordinary process of the law?"

"Naturally. It is attempted murder."

"And I'll have to appear—and all the rest of it?"

"I am afraid so."

The monk began walking about. Captain Vivien lit a cigarette and watched him.

"Padre, he is a homicidal maniac, with one man on his brain. If he is not charged, he is free. And he will not rest until he kills you."

The monk stopped. He said undecidedly:

"It would be sending him to hell. At least—— Couldn't one appeal to him?"

"It is only brute force and the law which appeal to him."

"He's got a soul somewhere."

"He has also got a devil."

There was a further interval of indecision. Then:

"One can't appeal to a handcuffed man. Would you take those off, if I asked you?"

Captain Vivien shrugged his shoulders:

"The Church of God asks it. Very well."

He knelt down and unlocked the handcuffs, replacing them in his pocket. Roslavl was groaning, as he did so. The monk came near. They saw the black slits of his eyes open. He looked vaguely about. Remembrance was returning. The black slits fastened first on the monk, and then on Captain Vivien who seemed to puzzle him for a moment. It must have slowly dawned on him in what capacity the latter was there, for he exhibited no gratitude when they helped him to sit up, but struck savagely at the flask in Captain Vivien's hand—a wild animal at bay. The flask was closed and put away. The monk was subjected to vile imprecations in Russian. The man was himself again amazingly soon. His hand even began to fumble instinctively.

The monk informed him:

"You'll find nothing there."

165

The man glared, impotently.

"How much English do you understand? I want to talk to you."

Roslavl muttered in Russian. Captain Vivien interposed:

"You can talk English, Roslavl. Come on."

The sound of his own name startled him. An alertness appeared. His cunning began to assert itself, though too obviously. He assumed incomprehension, surlily shaking his head, and then proceeded to stand on his feet. They let him.

He was warily waiting for a chance, for anything that his wits could turn to use. He began brushing at his clothes. The monk said slowly and distinctly:

"Roslavl, that's twice. Are you going to try again?"

He paused, almost imperceptibly, in the brushing process, and then continued. His self-possession was remarkable, considering what the question must have conveyed.

He took off his overcoat, and began shaking it—ostensibly to remove the dust and dirt. While doing so he looked about. He let go of the coat with one hand and pointed to his head, indicating that he had no hat. Captain Vivien went to pick up an object lying in the middle of the road. Roslavl followed. They failed to see his intention; and for once Captain Vivien was caught . . .

The full force of that kick might have broken his skull, had he stooped lower. As it was, it caught his temple at an angle.

"You devil!" came in rage from the monk.

Roslavl had calculated carefully; for already he was making for the corner. The monk flung off his overcoat, with the intention of running him down, realising, as he did so, that Captain Vivien was lying helpless in the centre of the road. He lost time badly dragging the dead weight to the bank, as Roslavl vanished to the left. He placed his overcoat beneath; and, in the act, became alive to something happening near by.

His ears had caught a shout, and then a hideous grinding of brakes. He remained still, on one knee, listening. A car had suddenly stopped. A woman's frightened shriek came. He saw the hedge across the main road whitely lit up . . .

Captain Vivien was stirring. He had not been more than stunned; and regained possession of his senses to perceive, uninformed, what had occurred. For his hand went straight to his temple. He looked about for Roslavl, and said weakly:

"So he has——"

"I don't know what's happened, yet. Will you be all right here?"

Without further delay—for more sounds were travelling on the night air—the monk went quickly to the corner and out into the main road. He looked down it to the left to be blinded by a dazzle of headlights. A car was at a standstill further on. He walked towards it, and must have been seen; for the figure of a woman, beckoning wildly, appeared in the stream of light. He reached her. She was in evening dress beneath a fur coat, and in a state bordering on hysteria. The left wheels of the car were in the bank. "Oh, my God! . . . Go and see! . . . I can't go there!" A man's voice called, "Could you come here, sir?"

The monk went on, past the car—to find a man on one knee in the road, bending over a huddled shape.

"Pretty bad, I'm afraid."

"What's happened?"

The man did not seem to know what had happened, beyond that a running figure had come swerving blindly into his lights, dazzled apparently. The car had caught him, and they had gone over his body, before he had time to pull up—"What the devil was he running——"

"Got a light? A torch?" the monk asked.

The man stood up shakily. He was also in evening clothes. He went back to the car. The monk stooped down.

He knew already whose silent form it was. His hands began feeling cautiously. Roslavl lay with his back to the road, his face twisted downwards, unnaturally. He lifted the right hand, and laid his fingers on the wrist. It was the hand that, twice, had held a revolver levelled at himself . . . He heard, "For God's sake, pull yourself together," to the woman, and the man returned. A thin beam of light played down.

"What do you make of him?"

"Hold it at his neck."

The little circle of white moved. The monk began unbuttoning. He succeeded in removing the collar.

"Looks queer? . . . What do you think? Get him on to a doctor?"

The monk informed him, "I am one," without looking up.

He began examining, inattentive to the man's remark. It took him less than a minute. His fingers merely confirmed what he had guessed from the position of the head. He took the torch for himself . . . The eyes were already glazing . . .

"He is dead?"

It was Captain Vivien, standing above him. The monk remained on one knee, his lips moving silently.

Then he raised himself:

"Yes."

CHAPTER XVII

§1

ABOVE THE DRONE of the Rosary a hymn began to rise and fall, stealing into the living hush of those thousands down below. From where she leaned against the stone balustrade, she could see a stream of colour moving slowly, approaching the head of the mighty inlaid cross which spanned the *Place*.

Verna watched.

On previous days she had been down there in the midst of it all with Terry. Today she had climbed the crescent to where it circled over the roof of the Rosary Church. It was cooler up here, though sun-scorched, as everywhere at Lourdes this week of May. It was not for the coolness, however, she had come—but to be alone. She had wanted desperately to be alone. Away from Terry and the others.

The volume of the hymn was growing; the van of the Procession cleaving a human avenue as it came—Mary's Children in their Lady's blue behind the crucifix. From this height they were a rivulet reflecting heaven above, flowing slowly nearer.

She watched the tiny veiled figures taking their places on the steps beneath, feeling poised in space and slightly dizzy looking down.

Men in black file came next, dividing and spreading across the *Place*, into position before the western front of the Church.

The black changed to a sea of colour, a blaze of emblems glinting to the sun, coming on and on—the multi-coloured banners of the nations borne aloft. She loved those banners, proclaiming allegiance to the Faith—the allegiance she herself, two weeks ago, had given. It was easier to pick them out from here—French, Belgian, Italian, German . . . battalion by battalion marching on . . .

The white of priests.
Then the gold of vestments.
There were murmurs behind her. *"Dio mio!"*. . . *"Le bon Dieu!"*. . . She drew in her breath as she saw that movement of the sick in the *Place*, running the whole length of the stretchers and chairs, as they raised themselves or turned their heads, ranked side by side all along. The multitude was kneeling, swept down as wheat before the wind.
The golden Canopy was resting at the Cross-head, sheltering the God of heaven and earth.

The bombardment opened as the hymn died down—that army of living souls crashing its artillery upon What was poised there, thundering back the Invocations as they came:

"Lord, we adore Thee!"
"Lord, we adore Thee!". . .

"Lord, we believe in Thee!"
"Lord, we believe in Thee!". . .

"Lord, we hope in Thee!"
"Lord, we hope in Thee!". . .

"Lord, we love Thee!"
"Lord, we love Thee!"...

"Hosanna, Hosanna to the Son of David!"
"Hosanna, Hosanna to the Son of David!"...

"Lord, he whom Thou lovest is sick!"
"Lord, he whom Thou lovest is sick!"...

"Lord, that I may see!"
"Lord, that I may see!"...

"Lord, that I may hear!"
"Lord, that I may hear!"...

"Lord, that I may walk!"
"Lord, that I may walk!"...

"Our Lady of Lourdes, pray for us!"
"Our Lady of Lourdes, pray for us!"...

Word by word, distinctly; language by language in turn, hurled forth passionately by those priests with the outstretched arms!

The Host was moving almost imperceptibly, down the lines of human wreckage, blessing halt and maimed, diseased and blind. She could see them leaning forward intensely as He stayed before passing on. She knew that to each one He gave something, and that sometimes He said, "Arise!" He had said, "Arise!" yesterday. And it had happened. She had been almost terrified. The monk had been with the Canopy, and had come forward to quiet the excitement of some Italians in the crowd. He was with the Canopy now, probably; one of that bodyguard.

Her attention began wandering—reverting to her precipitant action of an hour ago. She had insisted on seeing the monk at the Chapelle, taking her chance whilst others were waiting. He had only had five minutes. She had poured it all out quickly. He had listened, and then asked sternly, "You've not told this to Louis?" "No." "You've only just been received; anybody can imagine anything, at Lourdes." He had been almost impatient. She had wanted him to tell her that she was a fool, mad—anything. He had not done that. Instead, he had said, "You'd better come and see me again," in a more sympathetic tone. "When did this begin?" She had answered, "Months ago; when you were instructing me. I've laughed at it until now. I've simply said to myself—I'm going to marry Louis." His brow had furrowed. "Come here on Monday, after the Grotto . . . and tell Our Lady. Tell her everything". . .

The Canopy was passing before the façade of the Church, and coming directly beneath. She saw the group of brancardiers at the corner kneeling down. Louis was amongst them, somewhere.

The thought of him distracted her again. She was avoiding being alone with Louis, as far as possible. His brancardier's duties kept him during the day. In the evenings she had to make sure of Terry being with them for dinner at the hotel. Yesterday she had met him coming suddenly out of the Asile. A tongue-tied unnaturalness had come over her. There had been a question in his eyes, and she had only just succeeded in staving it off. Had he asked her, she could have said nothing. She *could* say nothing . . .

She made another attempt to concentrate on what was going on below; but a vivid memory of Louis was flooding in. A day in the country with him, when they had been to see the little old-fashioned house. Louis had been pale, with a weal on his temple. He had never told her the cause of that weal. She had gathered that something mysterious had happened, to do with the monk and himself—some danger that was over. She had had to remain mystified, but had thanked God for keeping Louis safe. She had argued against that first troubled stirring in her soul that God had kept him for her. For their married life together. Their married life . . .

A fierce resentment was suddenly sweeping up against this other thing—this clamouring, conflicting other thing within. Until those quietly spoken words had driven her in turmoil to the monk—to speak, as she had spoken, just now—she had been able, more or less, to suppress its vehemence. "I was going to marry Cyril," was all the blind girl had said. She had construed it into an intuition, for she had just told June, "I'm going to marry Captain Vivien, you know." It had startled, frightened her, coming like that—June had lost her Cyril at Archangel, in that hideous happening . . .

June had answered in that quiet, strange way . . .

She roused herself to the sight of the Canopy returning down the centre of the *Place*, and made a fierce effort to pull her attention back; despairingly, almost angrily. She had come here for some peace.

She was finding none.

A vast silence was descending, as on the terrace before the entrance to the Church, the Canopy came to rest.

She grew calmer. The mighty volume of the Latin hymns rolled up, stilling the tempest within. A bell rang from down beneath. She saw a tiny figure in white and gold raise the Monstrance for the Benediction . . .

There was a dead hush . . .

And then, unvoiced, her soul's prayer came:

"Lord, that I may see! . . . Lord, that I may hear! . . ."

She knew it, quite suddenly, on her way down the steps into the *Place*. Somehow, blind June Campion had guessed. She had hinted nothing, when they were together on the Pilgrimage journey out. Yet somehow, with her strange insight——

June would understand . . .

As though an angel had descended from heaven to assure her, she came face to face with the monk at the foot of the steps. He must have seen her and been waiting. He smiled and said quietly:

"Have a talk with June Campion, will you?"

Verna found her, after a search amongst the throng on the *Place*, talking with a brancardier at the gates of the Asile. She recognised the brancardier's back with its leather straps instantly. It was Louis.

She hesitated, waiting a little way off—aware that it was a strange thing for an engaged girl to do. She dared not trust herself to speak to him naturally.

He moved, and she saw his face; the clean-cut line of his chin, the familiar courteous smile, the immensely lovable quality in his bearing with blind June.

She loved him!

Loved him so utterly.

He turned and saw her; she was only ten yards away. He came to her immediately:

"My Verna."

She stood there, unable to move. There were people passing. He took her hand; but she drew it away. Her action bewildered him. She whispered piteously:

"Louis—some other time."

It hurt him, terribly.

"But—— It was 'some other time' yesterday . . . I do not understand."

"Please——"

June was coming in the direction of their voices, tapping her way with her stick.

"Louis, I can't—— You've to trust me."

She went forward to meet her, leaving him alone.

"June!"

The blind girl stopped and held out her hand. Verna slipped it through her arm, taking the stick.

"June, I've got to talk to you. I *must!*"

She led her without turning, in the direction of the Gardens. When she looked back, Louis was walking across the *Place* with his head down.

Away from the crowd, among the trees beyond the Asile, June said:

"You're crying, Verna . . . Tell me."

§ 2

Maimed and twisted, sightless and speechless—that tide of broken humanity surging round her feet. The slim, white statue in its rocky recess—Immaculate Mary poised between heaven and earth. Pilgrims endlessly filing in and out of the cavern beneath; clusters of candle-flames flickering in the wind. The brancardiers on duty, standing still and straight, or wheeling the sick to and from the Piscines. The blue-uniformed girls moving quietly amongst the stretchers and chairs. And all the while the incessant murmurous pleading of that throng. This tremendous organised daily routine before the Shrine. The strange absence of emotionalism.

Each day Verna had watched.

She had watched the sick being taken into the Piscines to be bathed, and brought out again. There was no particular excitement about them. Nothing apparently had happened. She had been told of one or two cures, but seen no *miraculés* with swarming crowds. The brancardiers were as matter-of-fact as railway porters. So were the Blue girls. Terry, who was one of them, had mentioned drily that it was "beastly hot work" with the sick. To a young American at their hotel, who had asked, "Say, what time do the miracles begin?" Terry had retorted, "You complete ass!"

It had been different, at first, from her expectation. All rather inexplicable. This atmosphere of matter-of-factness.

Last evening June had said, "Verna, we see ourselves at Lourdes." She had asked, "How?" June had replied: "Ask Our Lady at the Grotto," and then, "You'll understand yourself, my dear, when you understand Lourdes."

That was all the advice June had given her, though with an abundance of sympathy over the problem torturing her soul.

She had come here to the Grotto after the Torchlight Procession, in misery. Neither the monk nor June had helped her, as she had wanted help; they had neither of them expressed their opinion, in fact, virtually, refused to do so. She had wounded Louis, cruelly. A strong impulse had possessed her to go and find him: "Louis, I've been mad . . ." She had not done so. She had come to the Grotto instead. She had knelt, with her eyes wandering; unable to concentrate, with that ever-shifting crowd around. The slim white statue, in the dark above the candle-flames, had been aloof and distant—Immaculate Mary, still and silent. "Ask Our Lady at the Grotto." She had tried. She had obeyed the monk, "Tell Our Lady everything." She had tried to do that too; and finally had risen wearily.

And then, walking back through the *Place*, that quiet serenity had come; that sense of a tremendous Will. That serenity had been with her all today; at Mass; while she was making the Stations up the rugged, twisting hill. It was with her now.

She had been here for an hour already, since two o'clock, unaware of everything, except of what was going on.

The same routine.

The same—but different.

The sense of disappointment had gone.

The sense of futility.

It was difficult to analyse; but some obscuring veil had lifted. She was aware, dimly, of a new import—of a light dawning on this mighty work, so barren seemingly of visible results, outwardly so vast a waste of anguish and pleading.

It had been partly herself, her strung-up nerves, she knew now; but the completely cheerful brancardiers and Blue girls—who came here, year by year, to carry helpless cripples, bathe stenching bodies, tend open sores—were no longer rather irritatingly bright young things inexplicably doing what, to the natural man, could be nothing but loathsome and repugnant. It was not for the fun of it they came to Lourdes with their cheerios.

The very sick they tended seemed somehow different.

Half-an-hour ago she had talked with one of the sick.

A girl of twenty from Savoie. Stretched on her back, worn to a skeleton; great sunken eyes, her whole soul looking through. In health she would have been lovely. She was more lovely in the spiritual radiance shining through the emaciated frame. There was no defeat, but victory. Verna had experienced a sense of inferiority. The girl was perfectly happy.

Louis had passed them while they were talking; and they

had smiled at each other, as though nothing had happened yesterday. She had been thankful for that smile of Louis'. Last night, at dinner, it had been almost more than she could bear—that dumb pain in his eyes.

She could see him now from where she stood—making his way between the lines of stretchers beyond the Grotto. He was stopping before a young man huddled up on a chair. The young man put his arms round Louis' neck, to be lifted bodily; and she saw that the lower part of him was powerless.

She watched with her hand to her cheek.

Louis carried him, with the shrivelled legs dangling, through the lines to the entrance of the Grotto. The pilgrims passing inside made way. At the rock beneath the statue Louis stopped, and lowered his burden. The young man touched the rock with his lips . . . They came out on the nearer side, opposite to where she was standing, and then towards her up the passage-way—the cripple like a sack over Louis' shoulder with legs swinging grotesquely. Verna caught sight of the young man's face for a moment—and saw an unearthly radiance . . .

Her eyes were brimming. She was heedless of it . . .

Something was happening.

Something tremendous . . .

Something, in the presence of which the anguish of her own problem was fading into insignificance, gripping her innermost being.

She was seeing.

Seeing beneath.

The vast work of this human wreckage, pilgrims, brancardiers—all supernaturalised.

Knowing what June had meant!

Knowing too what the monk had meant:

This "War of the Cross".

This "volume of pain sweeping up, invested with infinite value, touched by the Cross of Christ". . . ."Calling down pity and mercy upon a world in darkness without."

Her ears had heard the words of his sermon in the Rosary Church at the time, but no more.

These "broken ones offering themselves".

These "chosen victims waging war against vice, immorality, revolt".

This "War of expiation"!

It was here, being waged all around her . . .

It came.

It came as a clear light comes.

Not vaguely, as the serenity had come.

Definitely.

Shaping itself consciously from what was going on before her eyes.

More than the sense of a tremendous Will.

She knew.

She knew what was being asked.

She knew, in that moment, most surely what was being asked of herself. . . .

By that tremendous Will . . .

"Mademoiselle!"

The voice startled her. The girl from Savoie was being wheeled by. She roused herself and went forward. The girl stretched out her hand, and she took it. The brancardier who was wheeling her stopped, and moved away for a moment from the stretcher. Verna bent over, and heard in French:

"I return tomorrow to Savoie. But I pray for you."

The sunken eyes, with their haunting spiritual beauty, were holding her own. Verna bent down, and kissed the thin, drawn cheek:

"Thank you so much. Please, will you?"

The girl whispered:

"Because I have watched you, when you look at the Grotto."

Next moment the brancardier was wheeling her on.

"Because I have watched you"?

Had she too, like June, guessed something? That child, broken on the wheel of life? So manifestly one of those the monk had meant: "God asks at Lourdes for victims . . . He chooses; you do not choose yourself"?

"You do not choose yourself"?

She was——

Herself?

She was anything but choosing herself.

It was Louis who had first wanted her to come to Lourdes.

Dear God!

Louis!

There came a wild surging of her heart.

On a stretcher? Yes.

A cripple? Yes.

But her health? Her strength? Her life?
Her all?
Her Louis?

There was no vagueness now . . .

She awakened to a movement about her. The steady murmuring of prayers had ceased. Stretchers and chairs were passing by—streaming to the *Place* for the Blessing of the Sick.

She moved back, apart from the surging crowd, and stood waiting until the way to the Grotto was clearing.

Then she looked at the slim, white statue above . . .

Her mind flashed back . . . to a November evening of last year, in London . . . the monk before that shop in Shaftesbury Avenue . . . that evil stalking naked and Satanic . . . The initial promptings of that tremendous Will . . . her change of outlook . . . her growing spiritual insight . . . a vision looming ever larger . . . thrust into the background from sheer fear . . . she knew it now—the fear of losing Louis . . . Louis, who, unwittingly, and by some inscrutable decree, had first set her feet upon this path . . . the whole long supernatural process by which she had been led . . .

Expiation?

Her eyes had not left Immaculate Mary.

Expiation?
She had never used that word to herself. Not even to the

monk. Or June. And yet——
   Had she always known deep down?

   She became aware of the emptied space before the Grotto;
of the guardian of the Shrine straightening candles.

   There was no compulsion.
   She was still free.
   She could choose.
   She could refuse . . .

   That tremendous Will?
   That tremendous Will pleading . . .

   She loved him.
   Loved him so utterly!

   Oh Louis! . . . My Louis!
   Mother of God! . . .

   Her face went white suddenly.
   She waited, steadying herself.

   Then, she went forward.
   And knelt there.

CHAPTER XVIII

FROM FAR DOWN below the song of Immaculate Mary was rising.

They could see, in the deepening twilight, the countless throng around the Grotto, the Procession emerging, torch-laden pilgrims ten deep, file upon file, a riot of light and melody streaming on.

They watched in silence the glittering river winding round the corner of the crescent, upwards towards where they stood on the terrace above the Rosary Church, a roaring torrent of sound—*Ave, Ave, Ave Maria!*—the unwearying haunting refrain, soaring to heaven, ceaselessly replenished by the oncoming tide. Each nation's banner aloft.

It was not until the golden flood of glory was flowing down the further side of the crescent that the monk moved, and leaned an elbow on the stone parapet in front. Captain Vivien had been leaning there for some time, with the light of the moving torches playing on his face. When his head at length turned, the monk knew the question that was coming:

"Padre, I have waited until this last night. Will you help me? It is about Verna."

The monk said quietly:

"I know," and added: "Verna came and talked to me this evening."

There was a slight movement.

"Something has happened? Is that not so?"

Captain Vivien's voice was not quite under control.

"Yes. Something has happened."

The monk waited.

"Louis, Verna wants me to make it easier. May I try?"

The other straightened himself from his leaning posture.

The monk saw the suspense in the eyes that met his own.

"Do you remember a letter of Verna's? On the morning when Roslavl watched?"

There was a nod in answer.

"Because I think it was beginning then . . . There was rather a curious postscript—about 'Louis' Devil'?" The monk asked, "You'd talked to her sometimes about a personal Devil, hadn't you?"

He was looking mystified.

"I suppose it had stuck somehow. Perhaps the Almighty intended it to. You'll understand in a minute. I'm trying to make it easier, you see."

"I am listening, Padre."

"'Louis' Devil' rather amused her at first. Did you know that?"

"I have thought so. Yes?"

"Can you understand her attention focussing—when 'Louis' Devil' came true?"

It was conveying nothing so far.

"Upon a living, personal Devil at work?"

It was certainly conveying nothing.

"But this—— Verna is different to me, Padre. She has changed."

The monk replied firmly:

"Verna loves you at this moment—utterly, Louis. That has never changed."

"Then what has happened?" came hoarsely.

The monk chose his words carefully:

"Something that seemed incomprehensible to her, just because of her love for you. I think, what the good God has intended should happen—at Lourdes." He hated it, but he had to:

"Verna came to me during the week. I was abrupt with her; I wasn't prepared. I listened this evening; I had to. You see, I could no longer believe she was imagining."

He plunged:

"Would Verna be likely, of herself, to imagine any life apart from yours—after——"

He broke off.

"Louis, I'm sorry."

He had seen the sudden dumb agony of realisation coming. She had asked of him a terribly hard task.

"Would you sooner I left the rest to Verna?"

There was no reply. The monk could almost feel the anguish of desolation creeping over that silent figure. Louis had loved with a great and faithful love, and waited through the years. He turned away his eyes. From his heart there went a swift prayer to the Mother whose song was rolling on, filling the night. *"Ave, Ave, Ave Maria."*

"It is the first time that I have known—this," came huskily.

The monk put an arm round his shoulders. The man, who moved unemotionally amidst crime and physical danger, was trembling.

"She's not chosen this for herself, Louis."

The other swallowed.

"I do not understand yet what it is—she has chosen."

"There's such a thing as—expiation?"

"Expiation?"

Captain Vivien was facing him:

"Not her life—for that!" broke from his lips.

"Yes. Her life."

The monk's quiet assertion left him dumb.

"Louis, I was startled too. Verna, with all her love for you, telling me this evening that it could not be—just because of something at the Grotto?"

"But, what has happened at the Grotto?"

The answer came slowly:

"I think, the understanding of a problem, of months."

"There is no problem, of which she speaks to me."

"She hardly could, considering."

"But, what problem?"

The monk thought.

"Verna sees human life desecrated by Satan. And she sees how a woman's life can atone."

"She could not speak to me?"

There was a note of sharpness in his voice now.

"Until she was sure that it was of God. No."

"And how is Verna—so sure?"

The monk felt a sense of helplessness. Louis' whole manner was stiffening. His affirmation, when it came, was disconcerting:

"Padre, Verna is always the idealist. And she is only a Catholic since three weeks."

"I know."

"You agree that it is—— She is in the first excitement, about the Faith which she has found?"

He did not wait for an answer.

"And it is what you say—she thinks a great deal about 'Louis' Devil', because I talk to her about the Devil who is behind the revolt in this world. So Verna, the idealist, says to herself that she must make reparation against the Devil—with her life."

"And not Almighty God?"

The direct question pulled him up. He faced it, however, with:

"It is very difficult for me to believe that Almighty God gives love—and then says, no . . . And I think also it is June Campion."

"You may discount June Campion," the monk replied. "Verna's going to talk to you herself; but she believes utterly—that God is asking for what He gave."

"As you believe it, Padre?"

The monk did not hesitate.

"Yes, as I believe it, Louis."

"And there is not self-delusion?"

"No. Nothing imaginary. Nothing about visions or voices, or anything of that kind."

It had little effect.

"But, *Verna?*. . . Padre!"

His tone was incredulous. The monk realised that he was not really listening. His normal, cool demeanour had gone. He was Louis, the lover, seizing at any straw.

They lapsed into silence.

The monk had no intention of pressing his own opinion. He had done what she had asked of him—broken it as best he could. It lay not between Louis and himself, but between these two and God.

Two figures were standing near the stone parapet on the further side. He had seen and recognised them a few minutes ago. He left Louis there, and went over. They turned at his step.

"June, why are you up here?"

She unlinked her arm from Terry's. Terry said something about coming back for her, and vanished.

"Verna's told me, Father."

The face lifted blindly to his own was troubled.

"So you know?"

She nodded.

"Does Terry?"

"I think she's guessed by now . . . Father, he must *not* think it's me."

The monk told her straight out:

"He thinks it's you partly," then made a hasty decision and asked her: "Could you disabuse him of the idea?"

"I can only tell him the truth. I did say something to Verna out of sympathy, when I saw what was going to happen."

"When you saw——"

"I did say that I was once going to marry Cyril—meaning that God had intervened."

The monk looked doubtful.

"Would Captain Vivien appreciate that?"

"He could appreciate that it was one woman's way with another, in face of what was coming."

"It was as plain as that? To you?"

"Yes."

The monk looked across to where Louis was leaning, with his face buried in his hands. She anticipated him with:

"He's taken it badly?"

"It's hardly an easy thing to accept," was his reply.

There was a pause. He asked:

"You've found him unapproachable, haven't you?"

"He misunderstood Verna turning to me."

The monk hesitated, considering. It would be better to dispel all false notions from Louis' mind. He knew that she would not see the relevance of it for a moment, but he said tentatively:

"There'd be no harm in your knowing that Captain Vivien was brought into touch with Cyril's death, the other day—in rather a strange way?"

She had started.

"June, a man was killed last winter on a road in Sussex. By accident. He was a Russian called Roslavl. Never mind how; but Captain Vivien identified him."

"Identified?"

"It was the man who crucified Cyril."

The blind girl remained very still. A painful distress spread slowly over her face. He wondered whether he should have told her, with the memory of it all still vivid. He saw her throat working. She said after a while:

"You want him to talk? To tell me the rest? Is that it?"

"Would you tell him the rest—about Cyril?"

She remained silent again. He could see that she was reluctant.

"Would you sacrifice your own feelings?. . . June, if he could understand!"

"How?"

"What was asked of you," he answered.

She understood then. After a moment she indicated with her hand:

"He's over there somewhere, isn't he? Will you take me?"

The monk was about to do so, when she asked:

"There's no doubt about her being accepted?"

"By a Contemplative Order? None, if it's from God."

June seemed to be pondering.

"She would——she would never see him again?"

"Once she had entered? No."

. . . . .

The spire behind had been illuminated in the darkening

night, and the terrace flooded with light. The monk had not noticed it.

He had left them together.

He was standing now, looking to where in the distance the torchlight flood was encircling the Gardens and shimmering nearer, returning towards the *Place*—a sunset's pathway on the ocean. . . .

The ending of the "Great Romance"!

On the face of it a cruel frustration; an arbitrary maiming of their love. Like the breaking of a beautiful thing. No angel from heaven had come down; Louis was being asked to accept almost blindly. He had lived and waited for his Paradise—for that Paradise to be snatched away.

"But, *Verna?*"

That cry of his heart had been the monk's own unspoken question, too. He could only guess the answer. He could conceive of God passing Verna by—had there been no Louis. The way of expiation *was*, humanly—inhuman. There were beautiful things broken on Calvary. A Mother's heart.

He wondered what was happening over there. They were standing, June with her hand on the stone-work, Louis apparently listening.

Whatever June could do, she could no more prove a spiritual experience than Verna herself. His own attempt had been, more or less, lost upon Louis; he had dismissed as purely imaginary Verna's notion of an expiatory vocation for herself.

"Not her life—for that!"

To Louis it was a wild impulse bred of idealism, suddenly thrust on him like this—a mad renunciation of her youth and loveliness, of all that the future had held in store. Those weeks of silent anguish, her whole long inward struggle, had been hidden from his sight . . .

"Father!"

He turned.

It was Terry. They regarded each other for a moment. He was aware for the first time of the blaze of light over the terrace. There was the same anxiety in her face that he had seen in June's.

"What exactly is happening?"

"How much do you know?" he asked.

"Only what I've surmised."

She would have to know some time—and it would be better from himself. He told her in a few short sentences the main facts, using the term "religious life". She listened with her head down. At the end she was perilously near tears. When she looked up it was to whisper pathetically what he had just said to himself:

"The ending of the Great Romance?"

"I'm afraid so."

She remained still.

"Poor Louis!"

She did not say, "Poor Verna!" Neither did she give any expression to her own feelings, although she was Verna's intimate friend.

"I've always felt something like this might happen."

"Have you?... Why?"

"I suppose, because it was the last thing that *would* happen." She added, "On the face of things."

He saw what she meant. The unlikeliness of it. The kind of unlikely thing God would do. To Louis its unlikeliness was sufficient for refusing to accept.

"Terry, did Verna ever talk about the praeternatural? To you, I mean?" There was more she had better know.

"The praeternatural?... No, I don't think so. Unless you'd include 'Louis' Devil'?"

He nodded. She regarded him in a puzzled way.

"Why, has 'Louis' Devil' anything to do with it?"

He told her.

Much what he had told Louis. She listened perplexedly. Whatever she had surmised, it had not been this.

"There's something about 'the world of this darkness'? Isn't there?"

"I'm afraid I've forgotten," she answered.

"Can you understand Verna seeing into the darkness? Louis' Devil at work?"

It was the word "expiation" that startled her. The full appreciation came almost as a shock.

"God does ask for victims, Terry."

He waited while she assimilated it. Her lips framed Louis' own question:

"*Verna?*... It seems so strange."

"To us. I know."

Her eyes were brimming. She looked away.

"Oh, Father, why has this happened?"

It was her very human feeling for them both. His own too.

"Expiation's a mysterious thing, Terry." He quoted half to himself, "'This kind is not cast out but by prayer and fasting'. You've not forgotten that? The unclean spirit?"

It arrested her. A light dawned slowly.

"Is that why Verna——"

She stopped short. He understood, and said simply:

"Perhaps."

And then:

"Why not?"

The golden river had reached the square.

He moved forward to watch, leaving Terry to herself. The oncoming tide was widening, swirling over the expanse below, a seething, eddying glory, rolling in, wave upon wave of light, the volume of its melody swelling as it came.

"*Ave, Ave, Ave Maria.*"

There were thousands with their torches still encircling the Gardens far away, while that blazing sea of symphony filled the *Place*, the sound of its song reverberating to the multitude above.

"*Ave, Ave, Ave Maria.*"

The monk was strangely stirred. It was the first time he had witnessed the scene from here. Verna and Louis were for the moment forgotten before the splendour of that vast pageant of the love of Mary.

There were English pilgrims in that throng to whom he had been preaching day by day; to whom he had preached that afternoon for the Pilgrimage's close. They would all of them leave this haven of the supernatural carrying something of its atmosphere away; something of its peace into the world's rebellious heart; something of the compassion of the Crucified to War-embittered, "peace"-embittered souls; the breath of Immaculate Mary into haunts of the unclean; something of the glory of God which transformed a Gethsemane of pain into a Garden of Resurrection whose very trees, the river, sun, were alive with the Divine.

These battalions would go forth, as others went forth ceaselessly, to conquer by their Faith a Faithless world. The Deathless Army of the Cross! Bearing the *lumen Christi* those myriad lights proclaimed . . .

The monk suddenly roused himself from his absorption, without quite knowing why; except from some disturbing sense.

A man was standing a few yards away to his left. He had been vaguely aware of his presence there. Only now was his attention arrested. He remembered, afterwards, noticing Louis leave June at the same moment.

The man's face was in the shadow, from the illuminated spire behind. He was apparently staring at the spectacle below. There was an unnatural tension about him, though, for which no engrossment could account.

The monk's faculties were all in a moment acutely alert. The man was staring—but neither seeing nor hearing. He was so certain of it that he moved nearer, and then went up to him. The man was muttering to himself, and did not turn at the touch upon his arm . . .

This tensity was no stroke.

His medical knowledge told him that. The hideous, repellent rigidness sent his hand to the crucifix beneath his habit. And, with his own instinctive action the priest in him awakened to the truth.

He was witnessing what he had witnessed once before at Lourdes.

The muttering lips were arguing and pleading alternately, with increasing fierceness.

The monk caught some Russian words. His brain was grappling with some familiarity, when the man turned swiftly. He knew him, even in that moment.

There was a frightened sound from Terry. The light had caught those glaring eyes and the mouth gibbering in terror before the driving of that unseen presence—the fingers clutching towards the crucifix held there, facing him . . .

If any doubt remained, that sight dispelled it.

The monk's lips moved. . . .

There was a malignant frenzy as the crucifix signed the space between them with a cross; and then an instant as though heaven and hell had clashed. . . .

The violence did not come.

Instead, the hands dropped, and the man went back. The distorted features relaxed. He stood there looking about vaguely, his face no longer working. Then his hand brushed over his eyes, and there was a choking sob.

The monk moved swiftly, and caught him as he swayed . . .

He was aware of Louis at his side.

The dazed man was leaning against him, held by his arm. Louis was staring into his face.

"Karenov!"

CHAPTER XIX

§ 1

I T WAS one o'clock in the morning.

The monk was not yet in bed. He was standing at the open window in his room at the Chapelle. There was peace in the night; in the star-lit vault of heaven; in the moon looking down on Lourdes.

And in the grey eyes a wistfulness.

A chapter in his life had ended.

And in a strangely unforeseen way. The Abbot's letter of the morning, recalling him to Issano, had appeared to cut across the work for which he had been asked and sent; and then, abruptly, the same night he had been given a glimpse of the Eternal Will completing the humanly incompleted—in two lives that had entered his own.

For, in Karenov, he seemed to see the completing of a plan.

Karenov lay asleep now in the next room.

He had just been in to look at him, sleeping the sleep of exhaustion, but also the sleep of a man whose soul was at peace. He had found it difficult to realise that it was Karenov lying there.

That this thing had really happened.

They had brought him down from the terrace—Louis and himself. He had been able to walk. Even to exercise his faculties normally. On the way down the hill the hymn of Immaculate Mary had given place to the chanting of the *Credo*. Karenov had stood for a moment to listen:

"I have believed always, in my heart."

At the Chapelle he had asked to remain there for the night. He had been still shaken, and afraid of being alone. The room next the monk's had been secured, and Louis had seen to the fetching of his things.

And in that room next door he had told them.

He had told them in a meandering, childish way—only now himself understanding fully what had come about, in the short space of that half hour on the terrace above the Rosary Church.

The monk was still wondering.

Not so much about Karenov, as Louis. He himself had suggested nothing to Louis. It was with Karenov's telling that Louis had seen the hand from heaven pointing, and the uncomprehending cry of his own heart answered. The first fruits of a great renunciation.

Karenov had been pathetically anxious that they should believe in his sincerity. He had not attempted to conceal the motive behind his presence in Lourdes—the childish, dogged policy of following the monk for anything against him; even for something with which to ridicule the miraculous. His presence on the terrace had been purely accidental. He had been directed up there.

That sight below had riveted his attention in a manner totally unexpected by himself.

He had been conscious at first of nothing but its grip; of a rush of boyhood memories of a religion that had once been his own. The vehemence of his sentiment had surprised him, and he had laughed at himself for a fool: those thousands carrying torches were emotionalists, drugged by the melody of their own song. It had not allayed his own emotion, however. He had fallen back on shibboleths—those of the Committee he served; by whom he would be paid for whatever he could supply against the very thing he was watching. The shibboleths somehow rang hollow, and failed to stem what was rising in his heart.

There was a reality confronting him that sneers could not submerge; something before which his own work appeared mean and shrivelled. Something refusing dismissal.

Something unconquerable.

And in that moment he had seen.

He had seen the Faith.

He had seen more. He had seen himself. He had seen the quality of that to which he had sold his soul; its intrinsic worth in face of that mighty manifestation of belief; the triumphant note of glory, that never marked the Revolution's Atheist processions through Leningrad's or Moscow's streets—those palpable caricatures expressing no conviction beyond the dull malice of Russia's Godless Youth . . .

It had happened then.

He could remember vaguely a figure stationing itself to his right, before becoming oblivious of his environment, insensible to everything but a hideous conflict within. The rest he had been unable to describe, except confusedly, with the horror of it in his eyes.

Karenov could only state that the struggle had been with no imaginary phantasy, but a living, Satanic personality, terrifying, overshadowing; who in that instant had sought possession of his being, urging, commanding that he carry on the task he had begun.

His soul had cried in agony to the God he had denied . . .

He had been aware of a crucifix, of that malevolent personality driving him to seize and break it . . . of the crucifix moving, and before his vision two streams of white light crossing . . .

So much Karenov had told them.

He had regarded, in a dazed way, the four of them who had been with him when he came to himself, looking from one to the other, before his eyes had finally come to rest on the monk, who was beside him with a hand upon his shoulder.

"I have seen you before?"

"Many times," the monk had replied.

Karenov had looked uncertain.

"In London."

He had known, then.

"You are the monk—Thornton."

He had become alive to the song of Immaculate Mary still ascending from the amphitheatre below.

"Tell me what has happened."

The monk had told him what he had witnessed. Karenov had listened, with twitching lips, the terror of it still upon him. He had remained quiet at the end. There had been something he could not quite understand, with the recognition that the other man was Captain Vivien of the French Intelligence.

"You know many things against me. What will you do?"

The monk had answered for them both:

"Nothing."

Even at the Chapelle he had scarcely been able to comprehend their attitude; mercy being, seemingly, a quality foreign to his twisted mentality. They had reassured him to be startled by a question implying his belief that Roslavl had somehow met his death at their hands—the monk acting in self-defence. He had been told the truth of that night in Sussex.

Karenov had done a thing, bringing home to the monk, as nothing else, the reality of what had come about.

It was no mere emotionalism, or remorse born of fear. He had knelt down before them, a heart-broken Judas, who had sold his Master hideously for mercenary gain. And then affirmed, without being asked, what he would do.

At six, this morning, the monk would be at the Rosary Church. For a penitent's confession.

They had persuaded him to try to sleep, and had left him. Louis had come with the monk in here.

He had handed him a box of cigarettes. Louis had taken one, and the monk had done the same. They had lit up, without speaking. He was waiting, wondering what Louis had made of it all.

"You do not ask me about June Campion?"

"Tell me," the monk had said.

It appeared that he had apologised to June—Verna had not been influenced. She had spoken of Cyril and herself. He had conceded that *le bon Dieu* did give love sometimes, and then say, no—in view of Major Rodney's martyrdom. But, with Verna and himself, it had still seemed incomprehensible. June had suggested that he accept without understanding. He had been obstinate, and replied that was arbitrary. She had been very firm—no, perhaps *le bon Dieu* could do more that way; that He was waiting for the complete renunciation, Louis' own acceptance as well. "Oh, it is difficult! . . . I ask our Lady of Lourdes—Tell Him, yes, I give to Him Verna; but I also ask, 'Lord, that I may see'—because I do it blindly, and I am unhappy." Louis had paused.

"And then the blind man sees Karenov and you, my Padre." He had come nearer.

"I am frightened, almost, when I see it."

The monk had asked:

"Did anything occur to you at the time?"

"I only know that a very great thing has happened . . . No, it is when Karenov has told us, now."

"What?"

"I have remembered then, 'Lord, that I may see'."

He had watched the other. The monk's face had conveyed nothing.

Louis had said quietly:

"Padre, it is a miracle of God—because of Verna?"

The monk had answered, then:

"I believed so the moment it happened."

He had sat down with pen and paper, later on, and Louis had remarked from the other end of the room, in a deliberately matter-of-fact tone:

"So you write to Verna."

"How do you know?"

"The manner is different when it is about someone who is present—and who is myself . . . It is a habit of the Intelligence Service."

The significance of the added sentence had not been lost upon the monk. Louis intended to remain with the French Intelligence. That other future was no more.

"And what is it you write to Verna?"

He was steadying his voice with an effort. The monk had replied, without turning:

"Something she asked me to let her know tonight. Would you take it to her, Louis? She's waiting up."

"Very well."

He had gone on writing. There had been the sound of a match striking; and then being dropped into an ash-tray. The cigarette had not been lit. The monk had finished the brief note.

"Padre ... at the Grotto—in the morning?... You will add that?"

The monk had understood, and hesitated.

"Wouldn't it be better from yourself?"

"Yes, if——"

The sentence had not been finished. Instead, a dreadful silence had come.

The monk had waited; and then risen and gone across. The other was standing with his head lowered, battling for self-control.

He had laid both his hands on Louis' shoulders.

Who had loved with an undying love.

§ 2

It was half past six when the monk came out of the Rosary Church with Karenov.

They stood on the steps for a minute looking over the *Place*. There was a crispness in the air. A number of people were crossing in the morning sun. An early butterfly flitted joyously by. Karenov said in a hushed voice:

"It is for the first time since many years that the world has been beautiful for me."

The monk removed his eyes from two figures passing in the direction of the Grotto—a man and a woman together, smiling to him as they went by—smiling bravely, so he thought.

"Because the work of the Committee has made life hideous," Karenov was saying.

The monk regarded him sideways. His face still wore a look of exhaustion, though he had slept for some hours. The grace of God was in his eyes, however, dispelling the furtive air. He saw him shudder slightly.

Chapter Nineteen

"You're not afraid? Now?"

Karenov shook his head.

"It is the memory—which remains."

"Of last night?"

"The monster is before last night."

The monk turned, facing him.

"The monster?"

"It is how he becomes."

Again, there was that slight shudder.

"Tell me."

He tried to explain:

"The work is for the Revolution, the Committee say. But the work becomes for Satan, at whom they laugh—'He is a myth'. They do not laugh when they are alone by themselves. He kills himself, one man, when he is alone." He was jerking it out emphatically. "Because always it is Satan—'You shall obey me. You shall make them hate God. You shall make them like the animals; like swine!'. . . Always he is the monster, who drives." He added, "I have laughed also, but not when I am alone."

The monk needed little convincing.

"I can believe you, Karenov."

He could very easily believe him, with the memory of Roslavl's insensate hatred of himself, the inhuman relentlessness behind. . . .

"Monster"?. . .

The monk looked at his watch. He was due to say his Mass at the Grotto at a quarter to seven.

"Come on."

He led him down the steps.

"Now listen, Karenov."

The other was informed briefly—they would return to the Chapelle for breakfast after the Mass, at which he would make his Communion; the Pilgrimage trains for England would leave an hour later, and there would be a place on one of them for himself—if he wished. He said at once:

"I go back to England. Please."

He was firm.

"To Russia, never. I cannot. Because it is not safe. I cannot!"

"Very good."

They went round to the left, making for the Grotto. In front, a hundred yards ahead, were the two who had smiled, walking slowly. The monk saw the woman slip her hand into the man's, and the man hold it for a moment without looking at her. Then they went on a little faster, with heads erect—bravely.

"I have not known—Captain Vivien is married?"

The monk instead of answering the question said:

"Karenov, I will tell you the story of those two, in the train."

Karenov turned a puzzled face. His curiosity was not allayed.

"They have children?"

"They have you, instead. When I tell you, you will understand."

Karenov lapsed into silence, mystified.

They passed the Piscines.

Round the corner the Grotto came into view, and a pilgrim crowd kneeling in the sunlight. At the altar, in the cavern beneath Immaculate Mary, a priest was finishing his Mass. The song of birds was all round and the sounds of the river and the trees.

The man and the woman were making their way towards the gates before the Shrine. The monk, picking his passage through the bowed figures, turned to find himself alone. Karenov had stopped, and was standing with his gaze riveted on the altar, lost to the world.

Chapter Nineteen

At the gates the man and woman were waiting. June and Terry were kneeling near by. The smile in his eyes, as he reached them, hid that which was in the monk's heart. He had travelled life's journey for a while with these four; from now onwards their ways lay apart.

He spoke to the watchman who guarded the Shrine. Karenov was admitted within.

Then he signed to the man and the woman.

They followed him in through the gates, beneath the rock of Immaculate Mary, where they knelt on the ground, side by side.

The monk for a moment delayed there—to bless two who had given their all.

There were tears in their eyes, as their lips touched his hand.

The tears of a great bravery.

ALSO BY FATHER DUDLEY

View a sample chapter from each title at www.staidanpress.com.

WILL MEN BE LIKE GODS? AND THE SHADOW ON THE EARTH

"Men, in their pursuit of happiness, are in danger of staking their all upon the greatest hoax ever foisted on humanity. This book has been written to expose the hoax together with the follies and fallacies of the hoaxers. In place of Utopian dreams the real solution of the problem of human happiness is offered."—*from the cover of Will Men Be Like Gods?, 1949 edition.*

Father Dudley's first two books on human happiness are published together here—his rare collection of essays together with the novel which introduces his most famous character, the Masterful Monk.

$15.00 — 216 pages. Available at amazon.com.

THE MASTERFUL MONK

"'Passion for freedom,' 'experience,' 'life.' There's nothing original in it. It's merely the modern method of excusing self-seeking."

Brother Anselm comes back to England to counter the Atheist's efforts to destroy the influence of Catholic morals. Between his lectures he is drawn into a struggle for the soul of Beauty Dethier, who is Catholic but fascinated by the "freedom" of the world and the Atheist. It will take more than argument to save her from disaster.

$18.00 — 342 pages. Available at amazon.com.

OTHER TITLES AVAILABLE FROM ST. AIDAN PRESS

THE QUEEN'S TRAGEDY, by Msgr. Robert Hugh Benson

"Upon the publication of former books of mine several kindly critics remarked that the reign of Mary Tudor told a very different story with regard to the Catholic character. It is that story which I am now attempting to set forth as honestly as I can."

$19.00 — 364 pages. Available at amazon.com.

THE NET, by Agnes Blundell

"Roger felt a freezing dew break out upon his forehead. The net was over him it seemed; in vain he told himself that he could establish his identity. His head was worth forty pounds to the vile creatures at the stair foot, and once in their clutches who knew if he could ever communicate with his friends?"

$16.00 — 264 pages. Available at amazon.com.

THEY MET ROBIN HOOD, by Agnes Blundell

Osmund does a good turn to one of Robin Hood's outlaws and makes friends with the band. But how can a band of outlaws help his family, robbed by a friend of Prince John?

$15.00 — 214 pages. Available at amazon.com.

REDROBES, by Fr. Neil Boyton, S.J.

Thirteen-year-old orphan Jacques gets into trouble in Quebec, and decides to run away to Huronia and become an interpreter for his Jesuit guardian, Father John Brebeuf. But his journey along the Iroquois-infested river may not be so easy as he hopes!

$17.00 — 300 pages. Available at amazon.com.

THE ANCHORHOLD, by Enid Dinnis

A chaplain's sermon drove Editha de Beauville to give up the world and enter the religious life. But could a strong-willed noblewoman accept and embrace full seclusion in an anchorhold? Read on to learn how she fared, and how her life affected those around her: Sir Aleric, her erstwhile suitor, now a crusader knight; Fr. Nicholas, a young priest who was quite bright, and thought so too; and Fiddlemee, the witty yet wise court jester whose past held a surprising secret.

$14.00 — 196 pages. Available at amazon.com.

THE ROAD TO SOMEWHERE, by Enid Dinnis

Richard and Ann discover a real Tudor house in London being sold cheap, complete with leather latch-strings, a tale of hidden treasure, and a wonderful piper. But will the treasure lose them the house and each other, or set them on the real road to Somewhere?

$10.00 — 106 pages. Available at amazon.com.

THE SHEPHERD OF WEEPINGWOLD, by Enid Dinnis

Sir Robert Luffkyn, rich grandson of a peasant, has purchased the manor of Weepingwold from the noble but impoverished de Lessels, intending to make the renamed Luffkynwold a busy center of his tanning trade. He sends Petronilla, last de Lessels, to Gracerood, intending her for its future Abbess, and plucks little Brother Kit from the cloister to become the new parson of the long-abandoned church. How will Father Kit fare with the parish and his own soul? What is Petronilla's true vocation? And is there really a witch in the parish?

$14.00 — 202 pages. Available at amazon.com.

SCOUTING FOR SECRET SERVICE, by Fr. Bernard F. J. Dooley

Frank and George are going to spend their summer vacation in the Adirondacks, thanks to Frank's uncle Ed. But once they get there, they realize something fishy is going on. Can they trust Pete, their Indian guide, or is he mixed up in it too? And is Frank's mysterious uncle really behind it all?

$14.00 — 188 pages. Available at amazon.com.

CANDLELIGHT ATTIC & ODD JOB'S, by Cecily Hallack

Here are seven true stories in honour of the Seven Joys of Our Blessed Lady, and ten more invented ones about the delightful Barnabas Job, to make a comfortable book for those who are afraid of the dark.

$14.00 — 192 pages. Available at amazon.com.

THE HAPPINESS OF FATHER HAPPÉ, by Cecily Hallack

Shingle Bay did not know what to make of Fr. Savinius Happé. He was a cheerful, rotund Franciscan, a famous author of books on everything from Etruscan civilization to Alpine meadows to beetles, and someone who had never quite mastered the English language. His jovial demeanor concealed a wisdom that alternately bewildered, astonished, but ultimately won over the people of Shingle Bay.

$10.00 — 112 pages. Available at amazon.com.

THREE RELIGIOUS REBELS, by M. Raymond, O.C.S.O.

"There must be men who give themselves to God, because there is a God who gave Himself to man." This is the story of three such men—St. Robert of Molesme, St. Alberic, and St. Stephen Harding.

$17.00 — 294 pages. Available at amazon.com.

THE RED INN OF SAINT LYPHAR, by Anna T. Sadlier

Once Saint Lyphar was a happy village in France, ruled by a generous

Marquis and taught by the good Curé. Now the Révolution has put the Curé to death, and the villagers are about to rise under the famous leader Jambe d'Argent. But a Revolutionary spy is lurking near the Inn. . . .

$13.00 — 168 pages. Available at amazon.com.

CON OF MISTY MOUNTAIN, by Mary T. Waggaman

"It had been a long night for Con. Just what had happened to him he was at first too dazed to know. Dennis had flung him into the smoking-room with no very gentle hand, turned the key and left him to himself. And, sinking down dully upon a rug that felt very soft and warm after the hard flight over the mountain, Con was glad to rest his bruised, aching limbs, his dizzy head, without any thought of what was to come upon him next."

$14.00 — 190 pages. Available at amazon.com.

NON-FICTION

THE AMERICAN HERESY, by Christopher Hollis

The history of Jeffersonian America and of its downfall is told here in the lives of four famous statesmen: Thomas Jefferson, John C. Calhoun, Abraham Lincoln, and Woodrow Wilson.

$18.00 — 358 pages. Available at amazon.com.

THE STORY OF THE WAR IN LA VENDÉE AND THE LITTLE CHOUANNERIE, by George J. Hill, M.A.

The story of the brave French Catholics who rose up in arms against the revolutionary government.

$18.00 — 342 pages. Available at amazon.com.

CATHOLICISM AND SCOTLAND, by Compton Mackenzie

The little known history of the Scots who sought to defend their country and their Faith from the onslaught of Protestantism.

$12.00 — 138 pages. Available at amazon.com.

DOMINICAN SAINTS, by the Novices of the Dominican House of Studies

The astonishing lives of fourteen saints of the Dominican Order.

$19.00 — 392 pages. Available at amazon.com.